Secrets of the Great Fire Tree

Justine Laismith

SECRETS OF THE GREAT FIRE TREE

© 2019 Justine Laismith

www.justinelaismith.wordpress.com

www.aurelialeo.com

Laismith, Justine

Secrets of the Great Fire Tree / by Justine Laismith 1st ed.

ISBN-13: 978-1-946024-32-9

Library of Congress Control Number: 2019938335

Editing by Leah T. Brown
Cover design by Lenny Wen
Book design by Inkstain Design Studio

Printed in the United States of America
First Edition:
10 9 8 7 6 5 4 3 2 1

SECRETS OF THE GREAT FIRE TREE

Glossary

Ah: An expression put before a name to signify familiarity. E.g., Uncle Liang is called Ah Liang by his friends or seniors.

Ahma: A word commonly used for someone employed to look after a child.

Ahyi: Auntie.

Cheung fun: White rice sheets rolled up; a common breakfast.

Choy: An expression used to fend off unlucky words so that they will not land on the person they are spoken to and consequently curse them.

Dumpling Festival: Also known as the Duanwu Festival or Dragon Boat Festival. It falls on the fifth day of the fifth lunar month. In China, it is a public holiday.

Ee-yr: Chinese expression equivalent to "Ew," used when encountering something disgusting or distasteful.

Ge ge: Big brother. Children are taught to address anyone older by rank; to call someone by their name is considered rude.

Guai: A frequently used Chinese word to praise children for being good and obedient.

Ha: "Prawn" and the laughing sound are homonyms; eating prawns signifies happiness.

Jie jie: Big sister. Children are taught to address anyone older by rank; to call someone by their name is considered rude.

Laoshi: Teacher.

Mala sauce: Traditional spicy sauce.

Mantou: Steamed white bread.

Pig's trotters: Usually served with black moss on top. The black moss signifies wealth, and the trotters signify hands; hence, eating the whole dish signifies holding wealth in your hands.

Soya sauce: In the far-east, soy sauce is called this.

Qigong: Internal energy that pugilists have, akin to "The Force" in Star Wars.

Qipao: Traditional Chinese dress.

Yu: In Mandarin, the words "excess" and "fish" are homonyms. Fish is used to signify a plentiful year.

In memory of my grandmother:
Yew Choy Heng

Chapter 1

Kai was in the pig enclosure, which was directly under his home—a square house on stilts that was the only hut on the steep hills.

His father, Lee, jumped down from the roof. The soil crunched. Lee went round the enclosure, shaking every stilt and panel. The ground would move if he shook any harder. "Come out of the pen, Kai. Yee Por's here. Go and greet her," Lee said.

Yee Por was the oldest person Kai knew. She lived on her own in the nearby hamlet. Reluctantly he rose to his feet and lifted the latch. A short way away from their hut underneath the plum tree, Yee Por was sitting on a coarse bench. Next to her, his mother, Mei, had her back to them, stuffing something into Lee's suitcase. Yee Por raised her hand to greet Kai, which made Mei look round. When she spotted him, she picked up something from the bench. Kai came closer, with Lee following behind. Close up he could see she was holding the necklace she always wore. The noon rays reflected its deep green, like the forest after the rain.

"This is for you." Mei closed the clasp round his neck. "This has looked after all of us. Now it will look after you."

Kai froze. Ma was giving him the heirloom? It was her grandmother's, who had declared that the magical charm had kept her alive despite being hunted by persecutors. It had protected Great-grandmother and it would protect her descendants. Ma loved that pendant.

"Mei! You don't have to give it to him!" Yee Por spoke in her usual raspy voice.

Mei knelt down in front of her. "Yee Por, I need to know that you'll both be safe. This looked after Grandmother. Now it will look after you."

"You're a big boy now, Kai," Lee said. "Ten years old already. You can take care of yourself now."

Yee Por waved her wrinkled hands as if a pesky fly was annoying her.

"Of course we'll be fine! Besides, we have the rest of the folks." Yee Por's bony arm outlined a circle in the air. "We look after one another, like we always do. You don't have to worry a thing." She turned to Kai. "You're a good boy. You'll come and stay with Yee Por and look after Yee Por, won't you?"

All at once, Kai grasped the finality of it. He grabbed Mei's blue sleeves. "Let me come with you!"

Mei got up. "Kai, be good."

"But why can't I come with you? WHY?" He knew he was being childish, but he did not want to be left behind.

"Because it's not allowed!" Lee raised his voice. He always managed to get cross with Kai even though he came home only once a year.

"WHY?"

"You *know* why!" Lee took a deep breath. "Ma's already explained to you. It's the law."

The reunion dinner on New Year's Eve was supposed to be a merry time. Everyone in China expected it. But it had to be his worst festive dinner ever. Pa had returned with the black piglet in his arms. Wearing a sick grin on his face, he had told Kai to take the piglet to the enclosure. At that moment, Kai realized he was responsible for Pink Belly's fate. Ma would not, could not, have done it otherwise, sneaking off with her at dawn. He even believed her when she suggested Pink had escaped. Ma would never betray him or her like that. Pink was his friend, not just a pig reared for slaughter.

Kai remembered when he first got her a year ago, the little piglet curled up in a brown box. Her head was black—so was the other end—but the middle was the color of plum blossoms.

"She's got a pink belly!" he had squealed.

Even though he was not supposed to name his piglets, the name stuck, like her marks on the ground when she pottered between the fence and her water trough. That was when the ground was soft and wet. But the rain stopped and the ground turned hard. Things changed after that.

This New Year's Eve, only a week ago, he had taken the black piglet into its new home. Ma had told him to be quick. He was supposed to put the new piglet in the pen and come up immediately. But the lumpy ground in the pig enclosure couldn't convince him to leave. He wanted to sit in the enclosure and soak in every memory of Pink Belly, even that familiar piggy scent that could only come from his friend. He remembered how this time last year when everything was dull, Pink Belly brightened up the place. This was her space, had been all year and would always be. In fact, he still half expected to see her scratching her back against the faded bamboo fencing.

The new piglet, Pink Belly's replacement, remained still in his box. He was black all over, like how Kai was feeling. What was Pa thinking? The new millennium might only be two years away, cities might be expanding, but black was still an unlucky color. How could he buy a black piglet, especially at this festive time of year?

Lee worked in the city and only came home on New Year's Eve.

This year was no different. He had never missed the reunion feast, which, judging from the smell of fried garlic in soya sauce, was about to start. Kai sucked the air until his lungs could not take any more. The sweet aroma teased his tongue. His stomach groaned.

He climbed up to his hut. It was a single room with a sunken hearth in the middle—sunken because you had to take a step down to be level with the fire. All the huts in the area were built like this— the fireplace a step down and surrounded by columns of wooden struts all the same height, like table legs. When a plank covered it, the fireplace doubled as a table. Today, there were so many dishes of meat and vegetables you could not even see the wooden top. Such a contrast to the year they had just endured.

Mei and Lee were putting the last dishes on the table. Instead of chairs, they simply stepped down toward the hearth and sat on the step.

"Ah, you're here! Good," Lee's bright voice made Kai cringe. How could he be so cheerful?

Mei was now piling Kai's bowl of rice with mushrooms and green stalks. At reunion dinner, to have a feast was a sign of prosperity.

Kai sat down, carefully tucking his feet in the gap between the struts but not so far in as to burn his toes against the heat of the burning coal.

"Ma, eat. Pa, eat." Kai addressed them as he had always been taught.

"Eat, eat! Here's to a happy and prosperous New Year!" Lee said.

"And a plentiful one!" Mei said.

"Yes, plentiful!" Lee singled out a slice of fish with his wooden chopsticks. It fell onto Kai's overflowing bowl just as he reached over. "Have some yu. Yes, it'll be a plentiful year."

Kai took up the fish immediately. Anything would be delicious, except the pork. Pink Belly's image flashed before him. Kai took a deep breath and forced himself to focus on eating. The braised fish slid down his throat; its saltiness enticing his taste buds. He shoved some rice in his mouth.

Lee selected a prawn swathed with sauce. "I'm going to have this ha." Noises of Lee sucking on the juices from the prawn shell followed. "Laughing hahaha," Lee said when he stopped for a moment. "That's why we eat ha during the New Year, so we'll be happy, like we are now. We are so happy now, Kai!"

Kai continued eating.

"Just tell him," Mei said.

"I know already." Some grains of rice fell out of Kai's mouth. He kept his head low to show them how he felt.

"You know why we'll have a plentiful year?" Lee glanced at Mei with a frown.

Because you made Ma sacrifice Pink Belly for the sake of this meal, Kai wanted to say. But even saying it was too hard, so he picked up a green stalk and put it in his mouth, followed by some rice, then another stalk, as if he were too busy eating to talk.

"Kai, let me ask you," Lee pointed to the enormous dish covered with black vegetables, "do you know why we have pigs' trotters?"

Pigs' trotters?

"Just tell him, Lee. Don't beat around the bush."

Kai slammed his chopsticks on the table. "They were Pink Belly's trotters!" Clumps of chewed rice flew out of his mouth.

"Kai!" Lee and Mei spoke together, the same threatening tone in their voices.

"What?" Of course he knew what. Slamming chopsticks on the table was rude. Angry shouting was bad luck. Pursing his lips, he chewed what food was left in his mouth.

"What's the matter with you?" Lee said. "I was just going to say, like this pig's trotter with the fortune vegetable, our hands have grabbed some luck too! Ma's got a job, and she starts straightaway."

Kai froze.

"If Ma doesn't take it, they'll give it to someone else."

They weren't talking about his old pig or her trotters. In fact, Pink Belly didn't even feature in their minds at all. Kai reached out for his cup and gulped some water.

"We don't have a choice. You know how bad it's been this last year." Mei put a mushroom on top of Lee's bowl. "And there might not be a job next year."

For a pulse beat, Kai was angry at the way they weren't even sorry about Pink Belly, but it was quashed by a burning question.

He forced it out. "What will Ma be doing?"

Lee spat out the prawn shell, except it was now a dried-out mesh. "Ma's going to be a nanny."

Kai ignored his ominous feeling. "So there'll be more food for us? And someone for me to play with?"

Mei usually answered his questions straightaway, but this time she paused. Kai shivered, even though they were sitting round the cozy hearth.

"Not exactly," Mei said. "He is not as lucky as you."

The room got colder.

"Who is he?" Kai asked.

"The young grandson of our Big Boss Da Laopan. He's about your age," Lee said.

"So we'll be moving to the city?" Kai looked at Lee, who looked at Mei. It was as if someone had died. Awkwardly, Kai stuffed some greens into his mouth.

"Ma will be," Lee finally said.

"You'll be staying with Yee Por," Mei said.

"At her house," Lee said.

The soft green stalks became corn cob hairs. Ma's leaving him for another boy his age? With the food still in his mouth, he put his chopsticks down. "I'm full now." He managed to mumble. Without waiting for their response, he got up and stumbled outside. The yellow light was fading. He wished he could disappear with it.

Things did not improve the next day. The New Year celebrations consisted of being around many grown-ups Kai did not know. People came to their place and they went to others' homes, like Yee Por's. Kai could tell some had been away working, like Pa. Getting festive red envelopes from these strangers was little comfort, even though they contained money. He would much rather be at home playing with his new piglet, particularly after what happened the previous night. He was in no mood for celebration.

He stayed close to Mei. "Ma, was Pa joking last night?" he whispered. Lee was within earshot from them, paying his respects to Yee Por.

Mei shook her head. "I'm afraid not, Kai. I didn't know anything about it either. Pa only told me when he came home yesterday." She leaned closer to him. "I know it's a big shock, but it's only for a year. Yee Por will be glad to have you. She's getting very old. It'll be good to have someone living with her."

"You'll be back after that?"

"No, you'll come to us then. You can't come now because there isn't a school yet. But they're building it, and it'll be ready for next year."

"Why don't they have schools in the city? I thought cities had everything."

"It's not that they don't, but you can't go to those schools because you were born here, not in the city."

The law that did not allow him to stay with his ma.

"I know." Mei pulled him toward her midriff and stroked his stubby hair. He buried his face into her tunic. "But it's like this everywhere. Parents go to work and leave their children behind."

"Can't you do something about it?" Kai said through the blue fabric.

"Like what? Change the law?" Lee scoffed.

Kai pushed away from Mei and glared at Lee. Mei pulled him back toward her.

"But Laopan understands our problem," Mei said. "Remember what I told you? He's building a school for his employees' children."

"And it'll be ready next year," Lee said.

"Yes, so you can come with us then," Mei said. "We'll have saved up enough money to pay for your school fees."

"It's only for a year," Yee Por said.

"And we'll call you at Uncle Liang's," Mei said. Uncle Liang was Yee Por's neighbor, and the only household in the area with a telephone.

Kai lifted his head. The mournful wind wiped the wetness in his eyes. "Why can't you *not* work for a year then? Why can't you wait till next year to start?"

"We've already told you," Lee said.

Mei's body moved and Kai found his face being held by her hands, one on each cheek. Her eyes bore into his. "Do you remember what it was like last year? Every mushroom you picked that we could not eat?"

He nodded, but he avoided her eyes.

"And when we even tried to see if we could eat the pearl fruit?"

He and Mei called it the pearl fruit, the fruit from a big tree near the river. They left dents on the ground when they dropped, which reminded them of the heavy pearls on a dragon's head that were put there to stop it from flying away. So they had named it the Dragon's Pearl Tree. This tree kept dropping its 'pearls' on the ground, which the birds never ate.

He nodded again.

"And only one cup of millet a day, remember? Even the piglet had not grown as much as he should have."

Kai winced. He had really thought they would keep Pink Belly alive for longer. He would have happily forgone the celebratory food and treats.

"We had to share so little food. Remember how you had no strength to fetch water? Without me, you'll have more to eat from our dried millet." Mei's pitch became higher; her voice uneven.

"Ma!"

"Listen, I'm going to need you to help me look after Little Piglet and feed it like you've always done." Her voice was a tone he recognized; a "that-is-that" tone, a "no-more-arguments" tone. He expected it from Lee, but not Mei. She was not usually like that. "I need you to do that for me, for us."

"This is your duty. Do your part for your family," Lee said.

Kai flared his nostrils and flashed his eyes, but Mei held his face firm.

"We'll come back and see you at our reunion dinner next year."

The reunion dinner next year. His eyes dampened. Quickly, he looked down and squeezed them shut.

"Come on, be strong," Lee said, putting one hand on each of Kai's shoulders. "We're doing this for you."

How can abandoning him for a whole year be for his sake? Kai broke free and dashed to the only place he knew he had a friend who understood. He slammed the gate.

Chapter 2

The breeze, reflecting his own approaching calm, had died down and the leaves had stopped swishing. Above him, he heard low voices and, yes, his mother sniffling.

"Mei, he's only a boy. He doesn't understand," Yee Por was saying.

"Even you agreed that a job like this was hard to come by." Kai recognized Lee's heartless voice. "An opening like this might never come again. Kai will be fine with Yee Por. And I've checked the house. It will withstand any wind and rain. It shouldn't give any trouble while we're away."

For the first time since it was uttered, Kai heard the words clearly. He had tuned out every time his parents said "while we're away."

"And I've…given him…the…jade pendant." Mei's halting voice. Kai looked at the pendant on his chest. He traced his finger over the character on the smooth stone.

"Yes, your sacred heirloom will protect him."

A plastic rustling sound, like a packet of something opening.

"Here, come on, you need this." Yee Por again. "And Liang has told Xinying to keep an eye out for him at school. She's head girl. He'll be fine."

"I know." There was a pause. "But a whole year!"

"It might not be a whole year, remember? Laopan has an old country cottage in Qiang. They sometimes go there in the summer. If they do, you can come back and visit."

"So you see, only till the summer, Mei. That's no time at all. You'll be back here before you know it."

"I know, but I can't help it. I'm going to miss him so much—"

"It's getting late. We've got to say goodbye to him or we'll miss the bus."

Footsteps. He saw the two shadows approaching. He snuggled up to the piglet.

"Kai?" Lee's voice.

"We're going now." Mei's voice came. "Please help Yee Por with the farm and the pig…and do your homework…we are relying on you, son."

"Study hard. We'll call you at Uncle Liang's." Lee's voice again.

Kai kept very still.

"Let's go. Let's not make this anymore painful," Lee finally said.

A deep sigh and footsteps moving away. Kai did not move. He could not move. Soon the silence became unbearable. Kai scrambled out of the pen and peered over the fence. Lee and Mei were making their way downhill. Every step they took he hoped they would stop and turn back again. Once or twice his mother glanced in his direction. He quickly ducked down. Even at that distance, through the gaps in the fencing he could see her face was unusually red.

Their backs neared the cluster of trees. Plants that grew on those otherwise bare trunks scaled the heights of the trees, weaving to form a veil—a mocking veil that now covered his mother's path from him.

The gate opened. Yee Por pried his hands from the fence and turned his palms upward. "Look at the imprints." Yee Por's throaty voice was the chorus of a hundred songbirds. "Let's go now. Let's get some of your things and go to my house."

She held the gate open for him. He let his feet drag further along the fence to the ladder. He wrenched himself up the steps, stumbled past the doorway with its empty hooks for drying maize. Inside, the walls were still decorated with festive red paper. The past week they had dined here together, like a proper family. Henceforth he would not see them until they returned in the summer or next year at the reunion dinner. The sudden enormity of time grabbed him, and he slumped to the floor next to the hearth with its three stones and empty pot.

His mouth was dry, but he could not bring himself to move. The more he sat there the more he thought about how much he wanted a drink. If he did not get any water down his throat, he was surely going to die. Perhaps he could just die and end this nightmare. So Kai lay down and waited. He got thirstier and thirstier, but he still wasn't dead yet.

Yee Por had finally locked the pig gate and climbed into the hut. "What happened?"

"I'm thirsty."

"Get a drink then!"

Yee Por spoke as if he were simply coming round for a few hours while Mei was in town selling herbs they had picked. Except Mei would come back later, usually with a treat for him, like a sugar-sculptured dragon.

"Drink it." A cup of water appeared in front of him.

Kai guzzled it down.

"Better?"

He nodded.

"Good." Yee Por took the cup from him. "You see? It's not so bad." She reached over to the hearth guard and leaned on it until she lowered herself next to him. "Just bring your overnight things, like when you came and stayed with me for the night."

Yee Por lived in the cluster of huts on the lower plains. Usually it only took Kai twenty minutes to sprint down to her house, but walking down with Yee Por was a different matter. They arrived an hour later. At least that was one hour less before Ma came back next year.

Like all the huts in the area, sun-dried maize used to adorn the outside of Yee Por's house when harvest was good. A stone hearth also sat in the middle of the room. The only difference was the noise. He could hear voices outside. From the chattering, it was a few people. They seemed to be coming closer.

"Yee Por? Kai?" A high-pitched voice floated in.

"Kai! Kai!" A chorus of varied high-pitched voices followed.

"Yee Por, are you there?" A man's voice called from outside.

Yee Por shuffled to the door. Kai lagged behind. Peeping out, he recognized the group standing below. They all lived in the same hamlet as Yee Por; Xinying, Uncle Liang, and a couple of younger children in the lower primary.

They all had baskets on their backs, even the little ones.

"We're going to see if we can help Kai move in."

"He's here already!" Yee Por nudged Kai to the door. "Say hello to Uncle Liang."

"You can walk with us to school tomorrow," Xinying said, swiping off a lock of hair in her face.

They walked the same way to school every day. She always had the two younger ones tagging along, and he always made sure he was ahead or behind them. After all, she was his senior; others would think he was groveling to her. As for the other two juniors, he would get teased for being a baby if he mixed with them. If he entered the school gates tomorrow with them, the other kids would certainly notice. It would not take long before the whole school knew.

Like when the other children found out Lee had left for the city years ago. A few of the boys had cornered him at recess.

"He left you when you were still in diapers?" It was loud enough to draw attention.

"You must've been bad to drive him away."

"He's not coming back, is he?" Everyone on the playground was watching by now.

"Does this mean you are the man of the house?"

Laughter, jeering ones. Then one of them grabbed his arm and gripped it hard. "This spindly weakling is the man of the house?"

Their words burnt more than the chilis that hung over his doorway. He could not wait for the end of the school day. Mei always met him on the route halfway home.

Life at school was hard enough then. What would they say when they find out Mei had also left?

Chapter 3

Obviously, Xinying was only offering to walk with him out of pity. Who would want to be around him when his own parents had abandoned him? So Kai simply nodded, making a mental note.

"Since you've moved in already, we'll head straight down to the river for water. Yee Por, do you need some?" Yee Por always relied on the villagers, especially Uncle Liang, for her water.

"No need. Lee's done it for me already."

The party made their way toward the river. They looked so happy, trekking over the hard path together as a family.

Unlike him. Left behind. With no family.

The hollowness in his midriff returned. He turned away from the door. Yee Por was already making her way toward the small pile of firewood in the far corner.

"Kai, can you go downstairs and fetch more wood for me?"

Unlike them, Yee Por did not rear pigs. She kept her spare firewood below her hut. Kai felt as if someone had squeezed his chest. He grabbed as many logs as he could and dashed back upstairs.

"Piglet's all alone." Kai dropped the wood by the hearth.

"He'll be fine." Yee Por arranged the wood in a crisscross manner.

"He's going to be lonely on his own."

"Do you normally sleep downstairs with him?" Yee Por asked.

"Noooo!"

"Then how will he know whether you are upstairs or here with me?" Yee Por lit a match. "I checked before we left. He's got food and water. He'll be fine for the night."

"Can I bring him here tomorrow?"

"No."

New Year's Eve in the pig enclosure flashed in front of him. "But we can't just leave him there! I promised I'd look after him."

After he left the reunion dinner in shock, he went to the only place he knew for comfort—the pig enclosure.

He crawled into the pig pen, tucked his head between his knees and huddled, ignoring the spilled rice all over his clothes. Kai shivered. He heard a movement in the box and turned his head. Against the buff cardboard two little charcoal ears appeared. A charcoal head followed, then the snout, which sniffed the air as if sniffing out danger. Then Pink Belly's new replacement crawled out of the box and sized Kai up; his little tongue popping in and out of his mouth. Unlike his old friend, this one had white legs, as if he were wearing white socks on his short legs. In that moment, Kai forgot his earlier disdains and wanted to pick him up.

He knew he had to be gentle. "Are you hungry?" Kai peeled the grains from his clothes and rolled them into a ball. With the rice on his open palm, he waited. The new piglet edged toward him. Kai stayed as still as he could, even when the piglet sniffed his hands and licked the rice off. Then Kai let him put his snout toward his wrists and breathed warm air up his sleeves. His belly was touching Kai's fingers. Instinctively, he curled and uncurled his fingers. The piglet stayed very still.

"You like your belly stroked?" He kept his voice soft.

A low, throaty grunt. Kai knew that meant he was happy. After a while, he rested on Kai's hand, so he picked him up and nuzzled him. The piglet's warm body made his ears tingle.

"This is your new home now. I'll take care of you."

Sniff, sniff, wriggle, wriggle, grunt, grunt.

Warmth from the piglet spread to his shoulders. "It's just me and you here from now on."

As if he detected an edge in Kai's voice, the piglet stiffened.

"I'll keep you safe, don't you worry," he whispered. "I'll make sure of it."

The piglet slumped back onto his shoulder. Sniff, sniff, wriggle, wriggle, grunt, grunt. At that moment, Kai made up his mind. "I'll never abandon you," Kai promised. "Or give you up, no matter how hungry I get."

He had made that promise to the piglet. "I promised I'd look after him, Yee Por," Kai repeated.

"He can't live downstairs. Didn't you see my chickens on the other side?" Yee Por said. Her voice softened. "On the way to school tomorrow, you can stop by and say hello. After school, you can go back and top off his food and water. You can still look after him from here."

After dinner, Yee Por pointed to the raised platform with a porcelain pillow on one side. "I sleep on this end; you sleep at the far end."

Kai looked at the other end. His eyes stung. On the wooden platform was a flat pillow. He climbed onto his mattress-less bed, his toes almost touching Yee Por's. Despite the sponge pillow, his head felt the hardness. Every part of his body cried until the heaviness that followed him all day finally pulled his eyelids down.

When he opened his eyes, it was still dark outside.

Chapter 4

A figure with white hair was bent over by the stove. Kai stumbled to the hearth, his body as rigid as the wooden bed.

"Come, have something to eat before you go to school." Yee Por held out the faded plastic bowl, her shaky arm threatening to undo her morning's hard work.

Kai grabbed it before the porridge spilled out.

He slurped a spoonful. It was watery and bland, unlike Mei's thick porridge. "I'll fetch water for us when I get back from school."

Yee Por smiled, showing all her black and white teeth and the gaps between. "Such a good boy, guai!"

Her porridge didn't taste that bad anymore. Yee Por reminded Kai of herbal soup. Here in the mountains, no matter what ailments you had, from the insides to the outsides, herbal soup was brewed and drank. The mysterious recipes were handed down from generation to generation. And Yee Por, like the soup, has been around for as long as he remembered.

Throughout the meal, he kept his ears alert. The sky was just turning purple when he finished. He gave the bowl a quick wash in the water basin and bade goodbye to Yee Por.

"So soon? But Xinying hasn't come by yet!"

Kai picked up his schoolbag. "I want to check on the piglet."

"Wait, Kai, you've not packed any lunch."

He had stopped packing lunch last year, around the time when the leaves turned yellow. If he brought lunch to school, there would not be enough porridge for dinner, Ma always said, no matter how much he complained that he was starving.

That must be the reason why Ma had left. He had driven her away with his constant whining. "I don't eat lunch, Yee Por," Kai murmured.

He made his way up the steep slope toward his hut and peered into the enclosure. The piglet was sleeping. A quick glance told him there was water in the trough. So he hurried along. School was still more than halfway away, even when he reached the top of the gradient. No little voices. He continued along the country path as if Ma were walking with him until he reached the spot where he would usually say goodbye to her, the section where she began her day's work. From this point on, he walked to school alone.

Voices twittered behind him downhill. They were only faint, which meant Xinying's party was still far away. Immediately, he picked up speed. If he increased the distance between them, he could pretend he did not hear them calling him.

As soon as he arrived, he climbed the stairs straight to his classroom. The teacher was looking at some papers. All the wooden chairs and tables were still empty. Kai got out his writing book. If he looked like he was working hard, the teacher would not ask him to go back down to the playground. He flipped it open to a fresh page.

A piece of paper fluttered out. It fell onto the floor face down. Kai picked it up and turned it over. It was a picture, drawn by both Mei and him. Whenever he could not settle down to do his homework, she would sit with him and play a drawing game. She would let him start the first shape; he always drew a square. Then she drew the second shape, usually a circle, and passed it back to him. In this way they took turns. Sometimes she laughed at what he turned the shapes into, sometimes he cringed at hers. By the time a picture finally emerged, he was ready to start his homework.

They did not get very far with the picture on this paper. On the left in unsteady lines were a hut and a boy running after his pig. On the right was a lady, drawn with many little details; a flower in her hair, a necklace, patterns on the dress, tiny lines and clouds to show she was running after them. Ma must have drawn this end. In between was just an empty gap, like the distance between him and Ma now.

Kai shoved it back into his bag and took out his pencil box, a coarse wooden box assembled hastily and cheaply. In it were his one pencil, one ruler, and one sharpener. He studied the squares of his writing book. His life was as empty as the blank pages. For the first time, he would much rather endure endless lines of writing than face the playground taunting. He picked up the pencil and marked a line on the box. First day at school without Ma.

Everyone was on the concrete playground at recess. Xinying policed the playground with a group of seniors. He pretended not to see her. Along the same side, another group was by the rusty see-saw challenging one another to walk from one end to the middle and down the other end without falling over. This group of children laughed and clapped as they took turns.

Ma had always wanted him to make friends.

He loitered by the low fence at the edge of the playground and glanced in their direction, as if the invisible force keeping him out could only be broken if one of them looked, or better still, smiled his way. But they ignored him.

There was a noise. The upper primary boys were round the other side where the back gate was. They had probably just sneaked into school. Being the only boy by the fence, Kai would be the first they'd pick on as soon as they came in. He was about to move away when he noticed Xinying marching toward the back gate. Was she going to confront them? There was a safer way to the back through the thick bushes. Hardly any sunlight penetrated through, so it was a damp path with decaying leaves. Nobody hung out there. He dived in and walked to the end of the path. Hidden, he peered through gaps in the hedge.

The boys stood in a circle. In the middle, a bird was on its back with its wing bent. About five other birds of the same type circled it. Every few seconds one hopped toward it, and the victim flapped its good wing at its antagonist, squawking as if its life depended on it.

"Awesome!"

"Wicked!"

"Wah, did you see that?"

Kai was thankful he had not eaten any lunch, otherwise he would have brought it back up again.

"That's cruel! How could you watch that?" Xinying pushed through the gap and stamped her feet on the ground. "Yah! Yah!"

The birds hopped away, then flew a little way and tried to come back for the victim, but Xinying kept shouting and stamping her feet. Kai was not sure what happened next. The boys took off for the back gate. Xinying was alone. The injured bird was not on the ground.

She dropped her lunch bag and ran after the boys. Kai squeezed out of the bushes in time to see one of the boys fling the wounded bird at a stray dog. The dog got up to its feet at once. The bird squawked but it could only flap its good wing. It stayed on the ground.

Xinying grabbed a stick. "Yah! Yah!"

But the dog did not move. She smacked the stick on the ground. The dog bared its teeth. Kai snatched up Xinying's lunch as he ran toward her. A half-eaten mantou smeared the inside of the plastic bag. He pulled it out and threw it at the dog. It landed less than a meter away. The dog gobbled it down and turned back to its prey.

"There's another one in the bag!" Xinying shouted. "Throw it further away!"

Kai tore the remaining mantou in half and lobbed it just out of the dog's reach. It leapt up and followed the trajectory; its spine nearly twisted the other way. Within a second, it recovered and ran to get its morsel. In a flash, Xinying picked up the bird and they both ran back to the gate. Kai turned the lock.

"Thanks, that was quick thinking," Xinying said.

"You were fearless."

"I just couldn't stand there and let them kill it." Xinying stroked the bird. It remained still in her hand.

"Sorry you lost your lunch."

"No, I'm glad you did it. I would have done the same had I thought of it."

"There's still half. Do you want it?" Kai held out the torn bread.

Xinying laughed. "At least I didn't lose all of it!"

The bell rang.

"I'm going to take the bird to the school nurse first. See you after school?" Before she turned down the corridor, Xinying threw him a smile.

"You just watch yourself, hero." Kai did not have to turn round to see who had just sneered into his ear.

Chapter 5

Even when Mei first started, the little master had trouble getting around. The mysterious illness had twisted his spine and made walking awkward. Once a day, Mei helped him outside to watch the sparrows flutter and hear the dogs bark. This activity tired him out.

Mei learned that just before the winter solstice, Dr. Chan, from the city in the north, was invited down. He gave Ah Sau, the family cook, a list of herbs with strict orders for their preparation. But up till now, the grandson was not any better. Dr. Chan was the latest of a list of specialists the family had consulted. So Mrs. Laopan decided to go to the temples.

Mei had not ventured out of the house since her arrival. Her only connection beyond the walls was Lee's daily account of the places he had driven Da Laopan. Since Lee was chauffeuring Mrs. Laopan to the temple, she asked Mei to come along. Ah Sau insisted on coming too, as they were stopping at the market along the way. She knew the best stalls to buy flowers, meat, and the whitest doves to present to the Gods.

Mrs. Laopan offered the joss sticks at the altar. Next she went outside to free the caged doves. Back in the temple, they headed to the counter at the far end. There were several open tins filled with flat wooden sticks. Mrs. Laopan asked the Gods for guidance and picked up a stick. The man at the counter signaled them to follow him. Down a narrow passageway, Mrs. Laopan swayed left to right with each step, her head almost touching the wall each time. Ah Sau followed behind. Mei tagged at the end until they reached a dingy room. After muttering that the temple elder would arrive shortly, the man disappeared.

Mrs. Laopan sat down straightaway on one of the two wooden stools. They were by the table with only a candle and a little pot holding three burning joss sticks. Ah Sau stood next to her. Mei waited outside. After all, she was the outsider. Ah Sau was as good as family, having worked for them since her son, Han, was in diapers. Now Han towered over everyone. Besides, there was no room for a second standing person.

Presently, the temple elder came.

"So this is your stick?"

Silence. Mei assumed he was reading the words on the stick.

"When was he born?"

"Sixth day of the seventh month in the Dragon year.

"Which hour?"

"Two hours before midnight."

Crash, clang, tang!

Pan scraping and metal ladle banging echoed from the dark corridor. Mei was so busy wincing at the noise that she did not notice Ah Sau at the doorway.

"Have you got the doctor's letters?"

Mei had forgotten she was holding Mrs. Laopan's bag. At once she fumbled for the stack of old medical notes and failed prescriptions. Ah Sau disappeared back into the room. Once more Mei was left in the corridor listening to the cacophony from the kitchen further down. This continued for several minutes. Then it died. She heard a man's voice.

"Time is tight, but you have a chance."

Chapter 6

After school, Kai was the first to dash downstairs and out of the gates before he bumped into any of those boys. Who knew what they would do to him for coming to Xinying's rescue. By this time, it was impossible to ignore the gnawing feeling of his empty stomach. He pushed himself hard until he reached the top end of the slopes. Ma used to meet him here after school.

His empty house greeted him with a clatter of trotters on metal. The piglet's snout stuck out of the empty water trough, a half-cylinder made of tin. He was trying to clamber out but kept sliding back to the middle again. Next to him was a small basin wedged in the middle of a rubber tire. It was filled with water.

Kai dropped his satchel and went inside. "How did you get in there?" He picked up the piglet and put him beside the tire. "This one is yours."

The piglet slurped up the water, splashing it over his white legs. When he had had enough, he looked up for a moment and headed back to the long metal trough.

"What're you doing there, you silly thing? You're not big enough yet."

But the piglet took no notice. He lifted his snout over the edge of the trough and then his front paws. His hind legs kicked and pushed until he dangled, with his middle balancing on the metal edge whilst his tiny front and back legs wriggled in the air. He fell back to the ground but got up immediately and started again. After a few times, he managed to pull himself over the edge and landed in the trough. Piglet stood there, as if he were stunned to have managed to climb over. Then he tried to get out.

Kai picked him up and tied a rope round him. "Come on, I've got to go back to Yee Por's. I'm starving!"

Yee Por was waiting for him. "How was school today?"

When Ma asked these questions, she looked at him with her water-chestnut eyes and school became a different place. He told the stories of masked men leaping from rooftops into school, or how he hid in the secret stone chamber in the principal's office and discovered ancient manuals of his forefathers. Mei never doubted his stories, as she asked many questions. Which dynasty were they from? Were there any pictures of his forefathers? Did Pa look like them? What did the manuals say?

Yee Por had a smile, but it was not like Ma's. So school was school, classroom was classroom, and schoolmates were bothersome boys; no heroes, no villains, and no secret chambers. Kai shrugged.

"You must be hungry. Come and eat," Yee Por said. On the table was a bowl of fluffy rice and a couple of dishes. "I've picked firewood, and we have enough water," Yee Por said. "Have you any homework?"

It was the first day back, so he had none. He wandered about with the piglet, but the usual games he played with the old pig did not seem fun anymore. They had only been fun because Ma was watching or listening. When it was dark, Yee Por told him to take the piglet back. Like the night before, he slept on the rigid bed. He shifted to get into a more comfortable position and felt something small hit the platform; the pendant Ma had given him. In the darkness, Kai felt the familiar blemish on the pendant. His mind went back to the conversation he had overheard on New Year's day.

"Lee! Mei! Happy New Year! How are you?" Yet another couple came up to them. Lee turned around and joined them.

"Bai! You've put on weight!" Pa said it to everyone he talked to. It was the etiquette to say that, as it meant they had been keeping well.

"No, I haven't, but you've put on weight!" Bai said. Turning to

Ma, he greeted her.

"Are you still working in the police station?" Ma asked.

"Yes, we're still at Qiang," the lady next to Bai said. "What about you?" But before Ma could reply, she pointed at Ma's new top and cooed. "That pendant goes really well with the blue top. Every year you wear something that matches your jade! How do you do it?"

"This old thing?" The pendant was shaped like the full moon but only the size of a star anise. "It's marked, not worth anything."

"I can't see any marks."

"Here, look." Ma flipped it to the other side. "Kai was very little when he scratched it."

"Ah, but even so, we don't see such lovely gems these days," Bai said. "Not in Qiang, anyway."

"Of course not, that's a rare one. Very unusual design," Mrs. Bai said.

"Well, that too, but also because the women are too afraid to wear them openly."

The lady widened her eyes and nodded. "The youths! They should be in school, but—" she shook her head. "Ai!"

"The whole place is going downhill," Bai said

Other strangers came up and joined in the circle.

Seeing he had an audience, Bai continued. "We've had an increase in cases at the police station—street fights, vandalism, or even worse, stealing public property!"

"What?" one stranger said.

"Yes, we've had road barriers stolen, can you believe that? Most people now avoid quiet lanes and stay indoors when it's dark; you never know when a gang of youths will appear carrying knives."

"They're all done by youths?" another stranger asked.

"What are they doing out in the streets?" the first stranger asked. "Shouldn't they be at home helping their parents?"

"Obviously their parents aren't strict enough," Pa said.

"It's not that. They're not around, the parents, that's the problem," Bai said. "All my cases were the same, they're left behind. Parents away working. Living on their own. Fending for themselves. Mind you, they start off good, doing chores after school, cooking, cleaning. Really good kids. But there's no one to steer them. In fact, one of the cases was only ten years old. Can you believe that? Ten years old, tagging along with his older brother, looking up to him, copying him. But who does his brother have to look up to? Not his absent parents, for sure!"

This caught Kai's attention. Ten years old? That's the same age as him.

"That's awful!" Kai heard someone say.

But at this moment, Ma moved away from the crowd, so Kai followed her. They were the only two edging away.

"Yes, I managed to convince Jian, that's the ten-year-old, to go back to school after the new year. But the older ones, ai, it's too late.

They won't listen," Bai said.

"Sounds like you know them all quite well," Pa said.

Kai turned round to see if Pa had noticed them, but Pa was still next to Bai, engrossed in the conversation. He caught one last bit before the drone in the room became indistinguishable.

"Well, there were a couple who kept coming back, like Jian's brother, with the scar down his face," Bai pointed to his eyebrow. "From the forehead, over his left eye and down his cheek," Bai traced the line of the scar downward with his finger. "I've questioned him a couple of times. You don't forget a face like that."

At this moment, a loud roar drowned the chatter in the hut. Kai caught a glimpse of a man with a mop of gray hair.

"Uncle Pak's here!" Uncle Liang's little ones ran out to greet the new visitor. "Wah! Uncle Pak! Is this your new truck? Can we have a ride in it, Uncle Pak?"

"Come, let's go and see Uncle Pak's new motor!" Lee ushered them out of Uncle Liang's house. "We'll say hello to him and then go home."

At long last all the visiting was done and most of the food eaten. Ma smoked the leftover pork, tied it, and hung it up in the rafters. Even though Pa was still at home—mending and repairing anything broken, like leaking roofs or doors that would not close—life had mostly returned to normal, so much so that Kai had convinced himself Ma wasn't really leaving.

But she left.

Tonight was two nights less before Ma came back. Kai scrunched his eyes to stem the flow.

"We need more water," Yee Por said after they had eaten the next day. "We've not had rain for a few days, the water butt's nearly empty."

"I thought you said we had enough water yesterday?"

"I did, but I forgot we need more now there're two of us and a pig," Yee Por said. "Uncle Liang brought a bucket of water already, but it's not enough."

Kai fetched his basket. It was wide and deep enough that if he curled himself into a ball, he could fit in it. Two pieces of cloths were tied to it in a loop shoulder length apart, forming the shoulder straps for him to carry the basket on his back. Yee Por held the basket for him while he threaded his arms through.

With the bucket inside and Piglet on a rope, Kai descended toward the thick bushes. Down the mountain path and past the soft green that grew around the clearing to his favorite Dragon's Pearl Tree, the tall tree with enormous fruit that went uneaten. To Kai, it was such a wasted effort; even more so last year when the tree tried to brighten up the dry season with heavy blossoms.

They were unusual flowers; instead of branches, they stuck out directly from the trunk. But like any flower, the petals fell and produced its fruit.

"The birds would not eat them, so we mustn't eat them either." He remembered what Ma had said.

Every tree and every rock down that familiar path to the river reminded him of Ma, how he used to charge ahead with Pink Belly, whacking the bushes and frolicking in the clearing until Ma caught up with them. Today, he did not feel like playing with the new piglet in the same way.

He had always gone with Ma to fetch the water. She was stronger and carried the bigger bucket. He carried the smaller one. It only took fifteen liters.

Without Ma, the road back was windier and more treacherous. The burden of the water weighed him down as he lumbered upward. Thank goodness Piglet was only tiny and seemed to know how to handle the uneven terrain, grass or rock, upward or downward. He rested his tired legs and shoulders every few meters. But each time he stopped, he listened for voices. He did not want to be caught resting by the school bullies. Especially now he was on his own.

On one of these breaks, he heard a rustle. Then a pair of huge feet appeared on the path.

Chapter 7

Kai glanced up.

Uncle Liang held a farming tool in each hand. "Is everything all right?"

"Just resting," he lied. His chest was still heaving.

"Ai, the water is heavy, especially going back up the mountain." He leaned his farming tools against a tree and dropped his back basket. "Come on, let's do a swap. You can carry my things."

Without waiting for an answer, Uncle emptied his basket. Kai gratefully accepted Uncle Liang's empty pot and bowl. It was easier to exchange the contents than the baskets as the cloth straps were adjusted to their bodies, not to mention Uncle Liang's basket was so big it would reach to Kai's knees. Compared to the water, the remains of Uncle Liang's lunch were weightless. They walked in silence until the steepest part was behind them.

"Xinying told me what you did yesterday," Uncle Liang said. "That was brave."

"Xinying was the brave one, tackling those boys on her own." He bit his lip. *I would not have done that if I were on my own*, he thought but did not admit it out loud. "I just made her lose her lunch."

Uncle Liang chuckled. "She said she couldn't have rescued it if not for you throwing her lunch at the dog."

Kai could not resist a smile.

"She brought it home yesterday. Its wing was broken, so we're keeping it until it's better."

They were nearly at Yee Por's hut.

"Yee Por's tank is empty again, isn't it? We could do with some rain," Uncle Liang said. "Then you won't have to go out again after your long day at school."

"Pig still needs to run about. The pen's too small for him to exercise."

Uncle Liang laughed. "Maybe you should let him carry some of the water." Uncle lifted the water bucket and pretended to balance it on the piglet's back. "I wonder if we can make a piglet-sized basket?"

For the second time since Ma left, Kai could not help grinning. He let Uncle Liang pour most of the water into Yee Por's water butt, leaving some to bring back for Pig.

"Come over to ours for a minute," Uncle said. "You can see how the bird is doing."

Unlike the aggressive squawk at school the previous day, it chirped in a soft tone.

Kai felt the same glow as when he was near Pig. "It's happy."

"And safe," Uncle Liang said. "Because of what you did."

Kai reached to stroke it. The bird lifted its beak and pecked his fingers. "Hey!"

"That's okay. It's just defensive. It's still feeling vulnerable." Uncle Liang spoke in a low tone. "Speak to it softly and move your finger slowly toward it."

Kai bent his head toward the bird. "Yes. It was attacked, five against one."

"Hurt by its own kind. It feels betrayed."

It was hard to ignore the ache in his chest. "Do you think it will ever fly again?"

"I hope so," Uncle Liang edged his forefinger closer. "We'll try our best to help it." Uncle Liang stroked its head. "It'll take some time."

The bird gave a soft chirp.

"You'll get better, little one, even though you feel abandoned at the moment." Uncle Liang turned and looked Kai in the eye.

Kai was sure Uncle Liang was only talking about the bird, but the words warmed him.

Back in the enclosure, Piglet went back to his metal trough climbing game. It occurred to Kai that he would always be stuck in there if he left things as they were, so he found a couple of large rocks. One he wedged in the soil. The flatter one he placed at the end of the half cylinder so that Piglet could step up closer to the edge. Then Kai sat back and watched his little game. Using the first rock, Piglet stepped up into the tin. Unable to climb out of the deep slippery tin, he trotted to the end with the flat rock, stepped on it, and climbed out. Then he went back to the beginning and climbed back in again. Once or twice he came and said hello to Kai.

When the sky turned orange, Kai got up. He stopped by his hut for a minute and then dashed downhill back to Yee Por's hut. The naked lightbulb was already on. He spotted Yee Por's silhouette by the doorway.

"What's that in your basket?" she called to him as he neared.

Kai climbed up the ladder and dropped his basket on the floor.

"You brought your mattress over?" Yee Por frowned, but her lips were curled upward.

"Yee Por, the wood is so hard!"

"Ai, your young bodies." Yee Por shook her head. "Can't take any hardship these days." When she smiled, her eyes blended with the lines on her face.

Chapter 8

"Time is tight?" Mei heard Mrs. Laopan's reply. "But Ah Fu's just very weak, isn't he?"

"For the moment, yes. Your grandson has an inner strength in him," the man said. "Whilst he is weakened by the fire, he is keeping it at bay."

Silence.

"Why isn't there a tree that's closer?"

"There used to be one near here, but they chopped it down to build factories. You're the first person to need it since."

Lee drove them back to the house. They whizzed past the open land. Not the kind of open land Mei was used to. Instead of trees, both sides of the road were lined with low but expansive barns. The only feature in the skyline was smoke belching out of long pipes that pointed upward. Mei could taste plastic as she inhaled the smog.

"The tree used to be there," Mrs. Laopan said.

Ah Sau nodded. Both of them gazed out of the window. Mei made a mental note to ask Lee about it when they were alone later.

"What did he say?" Da Laopan asked as soon as they walked in. The grandson was asleep on the daybed. Mei went over to turn him on his other side. Ah Sau headed for the kitchen.

"He's got a lot of fire in him." Mrs. Laopan sat down heavily on the cushioned chair. "It's burning him away." She let out a long breath. "The seeds of the Great Fire Tree, that's what we need, to cure him."

"Never heard of it," Laopan said.

"Remember the tree you chopped down?"

"The one the temple made a fuss over?"

Mrs. Laopan nodded. "Its seeds are brimming with energy, and they'll fight off his fire."

Laopan nodded. "Fight fire with fire. Did he give you the seeds?"

"No," Mrs. Laopan said, her voice parched. "Even if he had, it takes ages to prepare."

Ah Sau came back into the room with a pot of tea and served it to Mrs. Laopan, who gulped it down.

"It's a rare tree, not many grow in our area. The ones the temple knows about are down south by the borders," Mrs. Laopan said.

Mei had never seen anybody's face drain so quickly. "What is this tree?"

"I chopped it down," Da Laopan's voice was like weak pu-er tea.

"You mustn't blame yourself, Laopan," Ah Sau said. "It was the right thing to do for the business. It was in the wrong place, and its fruit can't be eaten. We all thought it was a useless tree."

"Did the temple man say where we can find another one?"

"Yes," Mrs. Laopan said. "The trouble is unless you know what the tree looks like, it's going to be impossible."

"What does it look like?" Mei asked.

"It's five stories high," Da Laopan said.

"Has large, green flowers," Mrs. Laopan said, "and they grow from the trunk."

Mei gasped. Mrs. Laopan raised her eyebrows, but Da Laopan was looking at Ah Sau.

"But Han will know," Da Laopan said.

"Yes, he should know," Ah Sau nodded.

"What's wrong, Mei?" Mrs. Laopan asked.

Chapter 9

Mei's thoughts flew to last year's hardship.

Despite many trips to the river, the maize, yam, and buckwheat had withered. The river levels had become so low there were no fish to catch. With less to eat, Kai had stopped running with his pig and begun to walk beside Mei. Maybe not running had given him more time to question things. As always, they passed under the Dragon's Pearl Tree one day. It might have been as tall as five plum trees, but it was a tree that the locals had learned to ignore.

On that particular day she had stopped and looked up. Even the tree's waxy leaves looked dull. Beside her, Kai picked up a 'pearl.' The fruit was as big as his head.

"Why don't we eat this?" Kai held it as far out as his weak arms could manage. "There're so many on the ground."

"That means the birds don't eat them either. That's always a sign."

"But the shell is so hard, they can't peck them open." Kai knocked the husk with his knuckles. It made a distant hollow sound. "See, Ma? So hard!"

He had picked up a large stone and handed it to Mei. She bashed the husk. It split open and several closed shells fell out. The broken husk was hard and almost dry, even on the inside. They knew straightaway it would not be edible. Kai picked up one of the fallen seeds; it was the size of his clenched fist and light. He tossed it in the air and caught it again. When he shook it, there was no sound.

Kai tapped it with his knuckles, then his nails. "What's inside?"

Mei thumped the shell with the stone. It cracked. At the same time, a gust of wind tossed her straight hair back. She closed her eyes and shuddered.

"That was strange," Mei said. "Did you smell that?"

Kai shook his head. He was facing her, so he would have been upwind if the shell had released any vapors.

"It was like almonds, but, I don't know, the wind blew it away too quickly."

Kai separated the split shells. The lining of sticky puree reminded him of the winter's sweet dough balls.

"The birds might eat them now," he said.

They left them among the fallen heart-shaped leaves and

headed toward the river. When they returned, a couple of birds had flown down to inspect this new entity. They were chirping away and hopping around the shell. Pig lunged forward, scattering the birds. They made a little flight over the cream puree and landed on the other side.

"Let's leave them alone. We'll come back tomorrow and see what happens," Mei said.

The next day and the day after, the white creamy puree remained untouched.

"I think I know the tree," Mei said at last.

Da Laopan and Ah Sau stared at Mei. "What?"

"Waxy green leaves?"

They nodded.

"Huge fruit, like a rough ball, dangling on thin twigs from the trunk?"

"That's right! You know the tree? Where?"

"In the forests where my son lives." Mei blinked away the damp in her eyes. "We never touched its fruit as the birds would not eat them."

"Sounds about right," Da Laopan said. "Nobody eats that fruit."

"It's because the heat is strong, too strong for any fires in our bodies." Mrs. Laopan sounded like she was mimicking the temple man.

"But you just said we fight Ah Fu's fire with its fire."

"It's an ancient tree. Its roots reach right down to the Earth's fire, absorb it, and pass it to the fruit." She took a deep breath. "A whole world's fire in a fruit, too potent to eat."

"Will it cure Ah Fu or kill him?"

"Cure him, of course! But we have to let its fire, or most of it, return to the Earth first."

"How do you do that?"

"It's all here, look. He's written it down for us."

Mrs. Laopan whipped out a folded rice paper from her pocket. Da Laopan read the long list of instructions. Halfway through, Mrs. Laopan whispered into his ears.

Da Laopan's eyes widened and he folded the paper.

"Let's get Han."

Chapter 10

That night in her cook's quarters, Ah Sau had three joss sticks between her palms instead of the usual one.

Han was folding a frayed gray shirt. "Wah, what's the occasion?"

Ah Sau moved her hands from her forehead, bowed respectfully, and pushed the sticks into the tightly packed joss ashes. Then she turned toward Han. "It's the first time you're going away on your own. I'm asking for your safe journey and swift return."

"Swift return?" Han fished out the copied instructions in his suitcase and scanned them. "Have you not read the procedure?"

"Of course I know. I was there, remember?" Ah Sau came away from the window. "I was going to talk to you about that."

She pulled out a rattan-weaved chair and patted the back of the other. "Sit down for a minute." She waited until Han was seated and leaning toward her. "I've known that temple man for years. He's always so dramatic. But I'm a cook, so I know. You really don't need to boil it for so long."

"But this isn't any tree."

"If you believe his tall tales." Ah Sau sighed. "Honestly, once overnight will do. I've brewed enough medicines for Ah Fu, I should know."

"But—"

"Look, Laopan and his wife can't think straight. They're too desperate to cure Ah Fu."

"Precisely! They are relying on me. I can't let them down."

"I know, I know, but they've tried so many doctors. Why would it be any different this time?" she continued in a whisper. "We know in our hearts he hasn't got long, even if we won't admit it openly."

Mei looked out of Ah Fu's window, mother and son were heading toward the main gates. She emerged from the other side of the courtyard carrying a blanket. "All set?"

"Just waiting for Lee," Han said.

"For your journey. From Mrs. Laopan." Mei handed over the blanket. "It might get chilly in the evenings." With her hands free, she fished out a shiny glass marble. "Can you give this to Kai when you see him please?"

Han took it from her. "He likes marbles?"

"He'll probably pretend it's something magical or powerful."

"Ah, yes, I used to do that too."

"You remember the way?" Mei asked. As least it would not take him as long to get there. Da Laopan was paying top fares for the quickest way.

Han nodded.

"Kai will be so pleased to show you the tree," Mei said enviously. She wished Laopan had asked Lee to go. After all, he knew where the tree was. But of course, Lee was only employed not too long ago, whereas Han was his trusted employee.

The familiar honk sounded in the distance. As promised, Da Laopan had sent Lee back from the office to take Han to the train station.

"Have you got your train tickets?" Ah Sau asked.

"Yes," Han was focused on the car coming toward them.

"And the bus ticket?"

"Yes, Ma."

The car stopped.

Ah Sau handed over the brown paper package she had been huddling. "Don't forget to eat. It's going to be a long journey."

Han took the package and climbed into the car.

"Do be careful," Ah Sau said. "The hooligan situation is getting worse."

Mei raised her eyebrows. As if reading her mind, Lee turned his head toward them and gave a little wave before putting his hand back on the steering wheel again.

"I'll be fine," Han said. The car began to move. "Bye, Ma!"

"Remember what I said! Be back soon!"

Together, they watched the car disappear round the corner.

"Oh, no!" Ah Sau's hand flew over her mouth. "I've forgotten to remind him about his clothes!"

Mei threw Ah Sau a questioning frown.

"I hope he remembers to change out of his city clothes before he arrives," Ah Sau said. "I don't want him to stand out, especially not when we know ruffians are everywhere. People will notice he is not from around there."

Mei decided Ah Sau, like an ignorant city dweller, had heard about one crime incident and assumed all rural areas were the same. But before she could raise the point, Ah Sau had already disappeared inside to burn an extra joss stick for Han. She shrugged it off as a mother's natural instinct to worry. Looking back later on, she realized it was in fact a mother's instinct that something bad was going to happen to her only son.

Chapter 11

There was only one bus to Pumi village. All the seats on the bus looked like someone had rubbed sand paper over them. Overhead, the handrail dangled with brown paper bags for those who could not stomach the jolts and judders of the country roads. Now that the morning sun no longer pierced through the windows, Han opened his eyes in time to see the bus finally coming to a stop. He staggered off the rickety bus.

Market stalls were set up in the square. People were passing in every direction, with food or homewares tucked in baskets on their backs. It dawned on Han that he would need a huge pot to boil the fruit. He sidestepped a puddle, headed for a homeware stall, and bought a couple.

"Come! Lai ah!" The man in the stall next door had such a

booming voice that Han nearly dropped his new pots. "The best crafts you can find!"

He looked over. Displayed neatly were bunches of green and brown crops he did not know the names of. But what caught his eye were some pretty embroidery and bamboo crockery on the side of the stall.

"My niece made these herself! See how fine her stitches are!" A set of eyes was looking at him. Unlike the threadbare, faded clothes of the rural folk, his 'tatty' clothes were clearly thicker and had a sheen to them. But the man's eyes were set slightly further apart than usual, making him look honest. Han trusted him instantly.

"Uncle, I'm looking for the little hamlet north of the Great Lake." He pointed to his right. "Is that the way to go?"

"There's nothing to see in that hamlet." The man put back the embroidery. "Tourists usually go to Qiang."

"Oh, no, no, no, someone has asked me to look for their son." Han moved out of the way as two ladies came looking at the bamboo plates. "He lives in that hamlet. Kai, do you know him?"

The honest eyes hardened and the eyelids lowered.

"I'll have this one." The taller lady picked up a plate.

The uncle looked away from Han and toward his customer, who handed some money to him. When he took the money, Han's eyes lingered on the man's hand.

"Do you know Lee and Mei?" Han asked when the customers

were gone. "Don't worry, they're both well. I'm just here on an errand for our boss. They told me Kai will be able to show me a place."

"What sort of place?" Uncle unzipped his waist pouch.

"Where a rare tree grows." Han continued to linger at the uncle's hands. His fingers were shorter in one hand. "The Great Fire Tree? Apparently the nearest one is somewhere here in this area."

"Never heard of it."

"Mei said she passes it on the way to the river. It's an unusual tree. The fruit dangles from the trunk."

"Oh, that one. Is that what it's called, the Great Fire Tree? I can show you where it is."

"Thanks, but I also need to find her son, Kai. Mei's asked me to bring him a present."

"Sure." He zipped up his pouch. "I live in that hamlet too. If you're not in a hurry, I'll take you when I'm done here."

"Do you know a Mr. Liang in that hamlet? I tried to call him, but I couldn't get through?"

Uncle broke into a smile. "That's me. Yes, there was a storm earlier in the week and the cables came down. They haven't been repaired yet."

While waiting for Uncle Liang to finish his sales, Han pottered around. A gentle breeze blew, tossing the market's scents into his nose. Sweet and spicy, roasted and steamed. After a while Han began to feel hungry. The mantou his mother packed had long since been eaten. He stopped by the dumpling stall and ordered several more. The peddler was more than happy to sell him her day's worth. Just as he finished paying, Uncle Liang came up to him. Together they left the town and headed toward the hamlet.

Without street signs, every path looked the same to Han. The valleys, despite the stony texture, looked cultivated. The intermittent canopy of trees danced and swayed in rhythm to the spring breeze. It seemed to him that they had been heading upward and upward. Finally, they came to a small cluster of huts.

"That's my house." Uncle Liang pointed to one of the huts. "But everyone's in the fields or in town, as it's market day."

Han concentrated on where to put his feet. The ground was a mix of stones, pebbles, and broken cement, with several potholes filled with dirty water. "Has it been raining all week?" Han stepped on a big stone.

"Yes, it's perfect for sowing now." Uncle Liang stopped.

Han looked up. They were outside the last hut. He looked back to where they had come from. Not side by side, but the huts were close enough to walk to one other.

"Yee Por?" Uncle Liang called. "There's someone here to see Kai." No answer.

Chapter 12

"Let's go up toward Lee and Mei's home," Uncle Liang said. "I think they'll be there."

Then Han spotted it. Even in the distance he could tell it was shabby. A strong gust could whip the stilts off the ground and send it tumbling down the precipitous slopes.

Standing by a dull wheelbarrow was a hunched lady passing a long plastic sheet to a child squatting down. The child spread the clear sheet over the soil and placed some stones over it. Then he moved on to the next row and dug holes in the sandy soil. The silver-haired lady followed behind and dropped seeds. A couple of birds hopped hopefully at a safe distance from them.

The woman's cloudy eyes rested on Han when they neared.

"This is Han," Uncle Liang said. "He also works for the man

who employs Lee and Mei. He's looking for the, what do you call it, Kai?" Uncle Liang looked at Kai, who was brushing soil over the seeds. "The Dragon's Pearl Tree? Apparently its real name is the Great Fire Tree. I offered to show him where it is, but he said he's got something for you."

On cue, Han took the marble from his pocket and put it in his palm. "Your ma asked me to bring this to you."

The words had the desired effect. The boy stood up. "Ma's sent me a present?"

"It's right here, look!" Han edged closer.

Kai stretched out his hand. "Ma got this for me?"

In the noon rays, the marble dazzled as vibrantly as the golden chain around his neck.

"Wah, look at that," Uncle Liang said. "Do you know what it is?"

Kai gave Uncle Liang a hesitant look.

Uncle Liang leaned toward him and whispered. "It looks magical."

The boy's face lit up like a lantern. "It is! It's a magical seed. It keeps the ground moist when there's a drought, but when there's too much rain, it soaks up the water."

Uncle Liang feigned amazement. "We'll never have to worry about the rainfall again!"

Kai beamed and turned to Han. "Did you know?"

"I didn't, but your ma said that you would know straightaway what it is." Han tossed a smile at Uncle Liang, silently thanking him.

He would not have found Kai easily in this place. He looked around him. Harsh rocks rose on one side. In the gaps between them, where uncultivated, lay fallen trees and telegraph poles. How was he going to stay here for any length of time?

"I know the tree." Kai interrupted his thoughts. "I can show you now."

Yee Por insisted on coming with them. That was how Kai's burden got heavier.

Chapter 13

The path toward the clearing meandered around huge rocks. Han and Kai trekked ahead on the uneven ground. Lagging behind, Yee Por moved in slow deliberate steps. Uncle Liang stayed with her.

"I can see it now!" Kai jumped and skipped, his right hand stretched out in front of him. "There it is!" He sprinted ahead toward a tree with a veil round its trunk.

Han craned his neck to grasp the dizzying height of the tree. "Yes, this is it."

"There're a few on the ground. How many do you want?" Kai said.

Han eyed the size of the fruit against the pots he had bought. "Four. Let's look for four of the best ones."

He let Kai drop them in, two in each pot. By then, Uncle Liang and Yee Por had caught up with them. Yee Por's breathing was as rapid as the stray dogs' in the market.

"Now we can bring them back," Han said.

"Didn't you say you needed to boil them?" Uncle Liang asked.

Han nodded. "And let them soak overnight."

"Do you have enough water?" Uncle Liang asked Kai and Yee Por.

They shook their heads side to side.

"Ai, should have asked you to bring your bucket too," Uncle Liang said. "Mine won't be big enough."

"Big enough for?" Han asked.

"Carrying water," Yee Por said. "You need a lot of water to boil all that."

It never occurred to Han that they did not have running water. He regarded his two pots. "I can fill both of these up and carry them back."

"You saw how uneven the paths are," Uncle Liang said. "But we can try."

They agreed that Han should carry only one pot of water. Kai would carry the other pot in his basket. They would carry the fruit by hand. Han went first and Kai followed behind, back the way they came but uphill this time. At one point, Han stepped down from a huge rock onto the grassy patch and strode off. About ten steps later, Han heard Kai's cry. At once Han turned round, in time to see Kai steadying himself against the side. Then he recovered and continued toward Han.

"My shirt's all wet. It's so cold!" Kai shivered.

"What happened?"

"I was just trying to get down," Kai said. "I took a big step and the ground suddenly appeared, and now I'm all wet."

"Must be the light playing tricks on you." Han squinted. In the dusk light, it was getting harder and harder to see how far back Uncle Liang and Yee Por were. Yee Por's legs looked like they were going as fast as they could, but each step was so small Han reckoned she needed to walk about ten paces to match his one stride. "Does she do this every day?"

The pair were now coming into sight.

"No," Kai said. "If we don't collect enough rainwater, I come here after school. But the weekends I make two trips, one to fetch the water and the other to do the laundry."

"You wash your own clothes?" Han thought of his own mother, who even made sure that his clothes were ironed.

"I've watched Ma. You just bash the clothes on the rocks."

By now Yee Por was holding Uncle Liang's hand. She stepped down the big drop where Kai had just spilt his water. She landed on the wet ground and let go of his hand. She stayed down.

Chapter 14

Han and Kai ran toward them. Uncle Liang squatted next to Yee Por.

"She's sprained her ankle," Uncle Liang said. "She can't walk anymore."

"Let me carry you on my back, Yee Por. I'm strong," Han said.

Uncle Liang saw Yee Por's doubtful look. "He is a strapping young man." He punched Han's upper arm. "Look at all these muscles!" He winked at Han and turned to Kai. "How's your internal energy?"

"My qigong?" Kai stuttered.

Inwardly, Han chuckled, recalling a fundamental fact about Kungfu fighters. They used their internal energy to push their enemies off balance without touching them. To ordinary people, they were simply moving their palms toward their adversaries in slow motion.

"I can't quite lift Yee Por to Han's shoulder," Uncle Liang said. "I just need you to use your qigong to lift her from the ground, just a little nudge."

"But I don't know how."

"Ah-Liang, stop messing about!" Yee Por said.

"It's not that hard, just follow my instructions." Uncle Liang did not seem to hear her. "Are you ready?"

Without prompting, Han bent down with his hands on his knees.

"Concentrate now, channel all your energy to your palm…that's right, I can feel it."

Out of the corner of his eye, Han caught Kai's intense focus, both his arms stretched in front, palms in a vertical position facing Yee Por.

"It's working. Wah, you're strong. I can lift Yee Por easily now!" Uncle Liang said.

To make it easier for Uncle Liang, Han bent even lower. Between the two men, they heaved Yee Por onto Han's back.

"Thanks, Kai." Uncle Liang's cheekbones were even more pronounced when he grinned.

Kai was fixed on his open palms. His face was so incredulous, Han had to look away.

"I couldn't have done this without you." Uncle Liang picked up Han's pot and they resumed their journey together. The shadows of the trees faded.

There was only one hearth at each hut, so Han had to boil a pot at Yee Por's. Before long, the cooking pot was hung over the roaring fire. Han and Liang bade goodnight to Kai and Yee Por, and then Han followed Uncle Liang back to boil the other pot at his place.

Long after the fire had died, Han lay on the wooden platform listening to Uncle Liang's snores. The moon had floated through the tree tops. He cocooned himself with the blanket Mei had given him, but it made little difference. He shivered from the earlier memory of using a small vat of cold water for washing. This was no country holiday. He thought of his soft feathered mattress. It was not as sumptuous as the boss', but compared to this it was luxury. Apart from cured meat hanging in the wooden beams, he could only see corn or millet to eat, unlike the fragrant rice to accompany roast duck, braised chicken, or even steamed fish his mother cooked. The thought of being stuck here for even another night was enough to weigh him down more than the pot of fruit in water.

The more he longed for sleep, the more his mind buzzed. How would he get out of this situation? His conversation with his mother kept coming back to him; the temple man exaggerates, boiling only one night will do. The seeds of confusion that were germinating in his mind since that night developed into a ripened decision as hard as his bed.

Finally he drifted off.

Chapter 15

Low whispers and gentle rustling in the room woke him. Han pried his eyes open. It was still dark. Silhouettes moved about. He sat up and grimaced. His spine has fused into a pole.

"Did we wake you?" Uncle Liang asked.

"Is it morning already?" Han arched until his back stopped muttering.

"For us it is. The children have to go to school."

Han scrambled up.

"You don't have to get up yet." Uncle Liang helped the little boy put on his coat. "They walk to school on their own. I'll bring you back to the river to fetch more water."

"Actually, there's been a change of plans." Han folded up his blanket.

From the back, a child started bawling.

Uncle Liang turned his head toward the back of the house and spoke louder. "What's happening?"

An older girl strode in. "Wen's not well. She's throwing up. I don't think she can go to school today."

Uncle Liang disappeared to the back. The wailing tunneled through the wooden cracks. He looked at the little boy, who had a frown on his face. The boy turned to the older girl.

"If Wen's not going to school, then I'm not going either!"

Uncle Liang reappeared. "Yes, Wen can't go to school today. You'll have to go without her."

"It's not fair!" The little boy stamped his feet.

"You'll catch that horrible germ if you stay at home." Uncle Liang put a schoolbag on the boy's shoulder. "Xinying, take Chuan to school now."

The girl dragged the protesting boy out of the house. Uncle Liang returned to the bawling patient. Han tucked his blanket into his bag and went to the hearth. When he lifted one of the pots, his arm nearly unhinged from his shoulder. Even with one pot sloshing down the mountain, it would be too cumbersome. Han bit his lips, he hadn't thought of this detail last night. There must be a way round this. He was not going to be stuck out here in this hovel because of a heavy pot of soaking fruit.

Mei's description suddenly came to the fore. The fruit was filled with light, closed shells, which were the seeds of the tree. He fished out a fruit and smashed it with one of the hearth stones. He pried open the husk and let its contents empty. The husk still felt heavy despite being emptied. The spilled closed shells were as brown as oyster sauce and lined with grooves. He put them back into the pot and did the same to the second fruit. Together they did not even fill up to a third of the pot.

"I'm going back today," Han said when Uncle Liang came back to the room. "With these."

"You're going to carry both pots?"

"Just this one. Two will be too hard to manage. I'll go and explain to Yee Por."

Wen, who had been quiet for this entire minute, cried again. Han was sure that Uncle Liang was not sorry to see him go. He thanked Uncle Liang and set out. The silhouettes of clouds had become the color of tangerines.

At Yee Por's hut, a pair of slumped shoulders and dull eyes greeted him.

"I thought you had school today," Han said, when he climbed into the hut

"Yee Por's foot is really swollen. She can't walk, so I'm looking after her today."

"I've told you there's no need. Just go to school!" a tired voice came from somewhere.

Kai glanced toward Yee Por's voice. He frowned and blinked

rapidly, then dropped his gaze to the ground. He did this a couple more times, deciding whether to heed Yee Por or not. In the end, he looked at Han and asked, "Have you come for the fruit?"

"Actually, I've come to say I'm leaving."

"So soon?" Yee Por's voice came closer.

"Yes, Yee Por." Han turned and nearly hit his head on the wooden strut. Yee Por hobbled out, one foot wearing a slipper, the other wrapped in cloth with her toes peeking out. The second toe on her right foot was curled up over the big one like she was permanently crossing her toe, wishing hard for something. He reached over to hold her hand and led her to the wooden stool Kai brought. "You must see the doctor if your foot doesn't get better."

"No need, no need. What can the doctors do with an old lady like me? See?" She pointed to the bundle at the end of her baggy trousers. "I've wrapped it up with ginger. That'll take the swelling down."

"How are you going to take the fruit back?" Kai asked.

"I can't carry all of them back, so I'm leaving these two with you."

"Can we eat it now?" Kai asked.

"I don't see why not," Han said. "Here, let me bash them open for you."

"Ma always said we can't, as the birds don't eat them. I wish I had thought to cook them first."

"Well," Han pulled out a folded paper from his pocket, "this is what I should really be doing."

He handed over the paper to Kai and waited.

"But Uncle Han, it says here that—"

"I know, I know, but I don't think we need to do that."

Kai let his head tilt sideways, but he remained silent.

"Of course if you really want to, maybe you can give it the proper treatment, follow every single step it says," Han said. "We've got the original at home, so you can keep this copy. And the pot too, a small token to say thank you for all your help."

Han climbed down the ladder. The sun was shining through the branches, casting early shadows on the ground

"Wait, do you know the way?"

"Yes, I'll be fine."

Chapter 16

With each downward step, Han took care to avoid spilling any water. The light was fading. The pot was heavier than when he had started. He wished he had had a better memory for the way back to the village; instead, he had ended up at the river.

Now he had to rely on the distant electric glow to guide him toward the village, except he knew he had already missed the last bus. He would need a place to rest for the night, but he did not trust his ability to backtrack to Uncle Liang's hamlet. From what he had seen on the day he arrived, he knew there were no inns at the village, so there was no point pushing forward. Ahead, a tiny plain sat above the protruding rocks. It looked flat enough for him to lie down for the night, and the grass would be softer than Uncle Liang's wooden bed.

He had eaten most of the dumplings he had bought at the market, save for a couple flattened ones. He consumed them in two bites. Still feeling hungry, he looked around him. Above him, the dried leaves rustled against the bare branches. In the shadow of the rocks, he saw some fungi growing on the ground. He could not tell if they were poisonous, so he decided not to risk it. His eyes came to rest on the pot he had been lugging, the seeds still immersed in water.

"At least I've got water," he said to himself. Looking inside, he counted how many seeds were in there. "I don't think they'll know if I ate one."

So he took one out, picked up a flat rock, and steadied it against the shell. Whomp! It cracked open, releasing an aromatic fragrance. Han breathed in deeply. Almonds, with something intoxicating.

Inside the shell it was lined with a paste as pale as soya bean curd. It was not as white as Mei had described, but Han put that down to the effects of cooking. His mouth moistened, and he felt his stomach churn in anticipation. Without hesitation, he scraped out the paste and licked his fingers. It tasted sweet.

Even before it was all gone, Han gave up the battle and closed his eyes.

Chapter 17

Kai watched Han trundle down the mountain. A couple of birds flew overhead chirping. "Ah! Ah! Ah!" as if they were laughing at his predicament. Eventually Han's silhouette disappeared, leaving only the lonely rows of plastic sheets on the mountainside. Even the birds had stopped their dawn chorus.

Feeling the smooth marble in his pocket, Kai tried to remember what he should do today. The morning rays were breaking through the clouds that covered the mountain peaks.

"Go to school! I'll be fine." Yee Por limped toward him with his school bag. "School is important."

Kai hesitated.

"Do as you're told! Go to school!"

Kai recognized that do-not-argue-with-me tone. "I'll be back as soon as school finishes. You rest, Yee Por. Don't do anything. I'll cook when I get home."

He knew he would miss the morning session now. He let his feet drag up the gradient. It would probably be recess by the time he arrived. Knowing he would have to explain to Laoshi, Kai rehearsed his speech as he dodged twigs stretching from the side. Tiny green shoots dotted the dead-looking branches. Spring was coming. That was supposed to be a sign of hope, but the only hope he had had gone down the mountain ages ago.

As he neared school, he saw the dreaded group of boys. They were strolling in the same direction. He clutched the marble in his pocket and slowed down to keep his distance from them.

But something made one of them turn around.

"Hey, it's the Hero, the Mighty Protector!" The others turned around. "Why don't we see your ma taking you to school anymore?"

Kai put one foot in front of the other. A couple of them strode toward him, a tall one and a stout one. He had not seen the stout boy in school for a while. They used to be in the same class. Kai even remembered that he was called Jian, the same name as the ten-year-old boy Uncle Bai talked about, but there was no time to ponder over the coincidence.

"Has she abandoned you too?" the tall boy said.

"Like your father?" Jian blocked Kai's path. "Did you pick up your uniform from the streets, you beggar?" Without waiting for an answer, he grabbed Kai's bag. "So what pitiful things have you got in here?" Kai let go of the marble in his pocket and pulled his bag with both hands, but the boy was too strong. For a heartbeat, he was glad the pendant was safely tucked under his buttoned shirt. As long as he did not get into a tussle and rip his shirt, the boys would not know it was there. So he let Jian empty the contents on the ground. "As I thought, just like its owner, rubbish, all worthless." He came up close and put his face right up to Kai's. "You're no hero, more like a beggar!"

He flung the bag down. It landed by the tall bully's feet. A piece of paper stuck out.

The tall boy must have seen Kai's reaction, for he grabbed it before Kai could get to it. "What's this?" He studied the paper. "Look, it's Ma's little boy going home with his precious pet. What a girlie picture!"

"Give it back!" It took all his energy to sound intimidating.

"Aw, is it precious? Did your ma draw it?"

"I said give it back!" Kai lunged forward, but the boy was quicker. He stretched his arm over Kai's head.

"If you want it," he crumpled it in one hand, "you'll have to get it." Then he swung his hand in a huge arc and the ball of paper flew down the steep side of the slope.

Kai ran down the slope after it. He had to get that drawing. Ma had drawn that picture with him. He pushed his legs hard as he dodged between the long grass among the trees and bushes. There it was, stuck between some bare branches. It was out of his reach. He shook the tree. It budged, so he shook harder. The scrunched-up drawing fell into his hands.

He teased it apart. *Rip.*

Kai drew in his breath. *It's only a small tear,* he told himself. *Keep going.* His hands shook. Anger rolled down his cheeks.

"Kai?" A familiar girl's voice.

Kai swiped his cheeks on each side of his sleeve and looked up. Xinying's face was flushed, and her chest heaving. Moving up and down with her shoulder was his bag and its contents. His parents had needed money to buy it, money Lee and Mei were away working for. Kai pictured Lee's disapproving look of Kai having nearly lost it and readied himself for a retort, as if Lee were scolding him. Xinying handed the satchel back to him.

"I was looking out for you." Deep breath. "You weren't in school." Deep intake of air. "I got it back for you."

"I don't need looking after." Kai grabbed it from her and shoved in the drawing. Hurt flickered across her black eyes. Slowly, she turned around and walked back the way she came. Thank you, he wanted to say, but the damage was done. So he turned toward the hamlet and plodded. With every step, he wrestled with himself. Maybe he should head back to school. Ma would be very upset if she knew he had skipped. When he was nearly at the gravelly path, he heard a twig snap. He swung round and scanned the open space. A little way back behind the cluster of trees, he spotted something white.

"I told you I did not need looking after!" As soon as he said the words, Kai realized he sounded harsher than he had intended, again. He hung his head.

Xinying came out from behind the tree and edged toward Kai.

"I just wanted to make sure you're alright." She stopped when she got close enough. "I know what it's like."

"How would you know?"

"They're like us." She walked toward him. "They're left behind too."

Kai gaped at her. Trying to digest her words, he brushed the dust off his satchel and opened it. The moment he pulled out his homework book, he knew she was wrong. "They're monsters." He straightened the creases of his writing book. "Look at this!"

"Uncle says they are really pitiful." She took out his pencil box and sat down on a gray rock by a tree. With the edge of her skirt, she wiped away the dust. "Their parents left for the city when they were still toddlers. Their grandparents died, so there's no one to look after them."

"Your uncle?" Kai's hands stopped on a page folded in threes.

She nodded, opening the pencil box. "Wen and Chuan are my cousins."

"No wonder they're nothing like you," he could not help saying.

Xinying chuckled. "They're still my family. And besides, they're so adorable." She picked up the broken pencil and sharpened it.

Kai sat down beside her. "Even when they are arguing?" He gave her a crooked smile and let his eyes drift toward the pencil shavings falling into his pencil box. In it, there was a piece of broken lead at the corner. He picked it up and made a mark on the box.

"What are you counting?" Xinying asked.

"The days my ma's away."

"I used to do that. But I've given up."

Kai felt like a whiny child. For the past few weeks all he had wanted to do was cry and shout and stop Ma from going. In contrast, this girl who he thought had been so content was just like him. "Thanks for fetching my things," he said. He really meant it. *And thanks for looking out for me,* he wanted to say.

Xinying peered inside his bag and pulled out the ball of paper. "They did this to your work?" Before Kai could nod his head, she tugged at it.

"Don't!" he cried. "You'll tear it!"

But Xinying's fingers moved in such a way that it loosened up enough for her to find the edges. Slowly, gingerly, she unraveled it and smoothed it out on her lap. Kai readied himself with retorts to her comments on the picture, but she simply handed it back to him and got to her feet. "Shall we go back to school again?"

He followed her cue, and together they played a game of stepping on the head of their short shadows as they walked back to school.

After school, Kai found the piglet's basin had already been filled with water. Nearby, he spotted Han's pot of fruit among the compost; a couple of the shells had been bashed open. Uncle Liang must have been here.

Upstairs, the table was empty. Yee Por was lying down.

"Back already?" Yee Por croaked. "Ai, I'm useless, not strong enough to get up and cook."

"Don't worry, Yee Por." Kai dropped his schoolbag. "I said I'll cook. You need to rest your leg."

Yee Por's eyes followed him, but Kai knew exactly what to do. He started the fire, measured out the cornmeal and water. Making porridge was not as simple as boiling the Dragon's Pearl fruit. As he stirred the pot, he could almost hear Ma's words gurgling with each stroke.

"When the water starts boiling, you've got to pay close attention. Stop it too soon and it'll be like water with hard bits in it. Leave it for too long and it becomes a claggy cake. Even worse, with brown bits stuck to the bottom."

Kai scooped up a ladleful and tilted it slightly over a bowl. As he gazed at the contents dribbling from spoon to bowl, a slow proud smile spread across his face. Not only could he prepare a meal, but now he knew what he had to do with the Dragon's Pearl fruit. They would not starve again, no matter how little rain fell. Ma could come home.

Chapter 18

By the time he helped Yee Por to the table, he had made up his mind.

"Yee Por, eat." Kai spooned the porridge into his mouth and his eyes nearly exploded. All he could do was inflate his cheeks, form a tiny hole with his mouth, and take deep breaths. He felt the burning sensation trickling inside his chest. "Wah, wah! So hot!"

"Skim off the top layer," Yee Por said. "Blow it. That'll cool it slightly."

He puffed at his spoonful of porridge.

"If you blow any harder, it'll fly into my bowl. What's the rush?"

"I'm going to the river."

"No need. We've got plenty of water."

"No, I need water to boil the fruit."

"But Han's left already."

"I know, but Yee Por, if it can treat a sick person, that means it can be eaten."

Yee Por shook her head. "I got Uncle Liang to open one of the shells earlier. I've been watching all day, but I haven't seen any birds eating it."

"That's because it's not ready. He gave me the proper instructions, so I know exactly what I have to do."

"What do they say?" Yee Por swallowed a spoonful. She swallowed another spoonful. The porridge temperature did not seem to bother her.

"It has to be boiled and soaked overnight five times."

"Five times? Carrying all that water back for five nights?"

"I don't mind, if it means we can eat it. I would even do it ten times if it said so"

For once Yee Por let the porridge remain in her mouth for more than three counts while she thought. She swallowed her porridge. "If you want to do it, and you have to do it for five nights, it makes more sense to boil it by the river. It'll save you all that carrying."

Yee Por listened like Ma, and gave suggestions like Ma too. And she was right. Kai beamed at her and guzzled down his remaining porridge. There was not a moment to lose. He washed up, took a box of matches, his water bucket, Han's pot, and stuffed them into his basket.

Like old times, he ran toward the river with Pig trailing behind.

When he arrived, his pounding heart almost broke through his ribs. His leg muscles tightened and the bones were about to snap. He sunk down on the soft grass and leaned back against the tree. He was so busy gulping the air that he did not hear the chattering further down the river.

Pig trotted up from behind and gave him a little nudge. Kai turned his head to greet his friend. In response, Pig licked his wet face.

"Stop it!" Kai moved his face side to side to avoid the slobbery display of affection. He rolled over on the grass and faced downward, but Pig wasn't having any of it. The piglet nudged him on his side, right under his ribs. He jerked. "Oi, that tickles. Stop it!" In the end, the only way to get away from Pig's drool was to get up and fill the pot with water. Then he picked up one of the fallen fruit.

"Hello!"

Kai tensed up and looked about him. Downstream, a tall girl was coming toward him.

"What are you doing here?" he asked, almost rudely. This section was his river, only he and Ma came here. No one else.

As she came closer, he realized it was Xinying. He had not recognized her without her school uniform.

"Oh, it's you," he said in a friendlier voice. "Why are you here?"

"Washing our clothes," she said. "See further down there, beyond the bend?" She pointed to where the river disappeared behind a cluster of trees. "That's our washing spot. There're lots of big rocks to lay out the clothes. I usually come on the weekend, but we were busy sowing." She looked at the fruit between his hands. "What are you doing with the football fruit?"

"Football fruit?" He ran his fingers over its uneven exterior.

Xinying laughed. "We didn't know its real name. That's what we called it until Uncle Han came."

"You play football with it?"

"Not exactly, it's so heavy. We just kick it to see how far we can make it roll."

Kai put it back on the ground and kicked it. It almost reached Xinying's feet. He grinned. "How far can Wen and Chuan kick?"

She shrugged. "They've not tried it, I only do that with my friends while we wait for our clothes to dry. Keeps us warm when it's cold and windy."

"Xinying, where are you? We're going now!" a shrill voice penetrated from downstream.

"You go ahead, I'll catch up!" Xinying called back.

"Why? What are you doing?" Her friend's voice became louder.

Xinying hurried down and disappeared. He was alone again. Kai picked up the fruit. It was as heavy as his disappointment. He was about to turn back toward the pot when he heard her voice again.

"There, I've got rid of them for you." She breezed toward him. "So, are you playing football with your pig?"

Kai laughed. He recounted the temple man's instructions and

watched her eyes grow wide.

"Can I help you?" she asked. When she smiled, a dimple on her left cheek seemed to light her eyes. "I can gather the firewood for you."

Kai felt like he had grown two inches.

Xinying foraged for the driest firewood while Kai built a scaffold for the pot. He followed Han's method and cracked the husk with a rock. Six fruits' worth of closed shells were emptied into the pot of water.

Once or twice he looked toward Xinying's direction, wondering if he should say something, but she was focused on her job. Apart from little words like "Thank you" or "Careful" they had not really spoken very much. Whenever the wind picked up, Xinying tossed her head in its direction, to let her hair flow the breeze. He relaxed.

Soon the fire wrapped around the pot and the water bubbled steadily. Under his coat, the golden chain branded his skin. Even the jade was beginning to feel warm. Kai unzipped his jacket.

Xinying wiped perspiration off her forehead with the back of her right hand and unzipped her jacket too. "I'd better go back now. I've still got to make dinner," she said.

While she put away the dried clothes in her basket, Kai refilled his bucket with more water. When the basket was secure on his back, Xinying lifted his bucket of water and placed it in. Together, they started their journey back.

The next day after school, he set off with Pig to the riverbank.

Xinying was already there, idly stirring the nuts. Pig pottered up and sniffed the pot. Xinying reached over and stroked him. He smiled at her.

"Are you ready?" he asked.

Xinying got to her feet. In synchrony, they counted to three, lifted the pot off the scaffold, and plonked it down. The ground shook so much Pig ran off, especially when they pushed the pot over in his direction. The seeds gushed out with the water. Xinying took the pot to the river and re-filled it while Kai arranged the twigs he had picked along the way. Pig scurried backward and forward between the two of them. It was a great game. By now the big pot was filled. Kai lit the fire, then both of them lay down, exhausted. Pig lay on the cool patch where they had emptied the water earlier.

For the next four days they met by the river late in the afternoon after they had completed their chores.

"What did you cook today?" Kai asked Xinying when they met up.

"Garlic stalks." She broke off a long dried twig from a tree. "They're in season again."

"Oh, I love those!"

"Yes, Uncle said that too. He bought some extra for you. I'll bring some over when we get back. Uncle bought more than this lot from the market today!" She held her arms out and dropped an armful of twigs on the ground. "Sometimes he thinks we eat as much as him."

"But you eat even less than a little bird."

"Exactly!" Her eyes lit up. "Oh, it's almost ready to fly again."

Kai frowned. Then he beamed. "The bird from school? I didn't think it would even survive. You're so clever, looking after it."

"Not really. Uncle showed me."

Kai put the shells back into the pot with fresh water. "So both your parents are away too?" He tried to sound casual.

"They've been away for a long time." Her lips stuck out. She added more twigs to the pile of burned out wood. "They left before I started school."

"Wah, since kindergarten?"

"I still remember that day." She fished a box of matches from her pocket. "Ma had a huge bundle with her. She said she was going to the market to sell mushrooms." Xinying gave a little snort. "I remember being pleased that we had picked so many mushrooms to sell. I even waved goodbye to her."

"How did you find out?"

"She did not come back that night. I kept asking when she'd be back. Ahyi told me to go to sleep and see what happens in the morning." Xinying struck the match. "So I did. When I woke up, she wasn't back. I asked Ahyi again." She held the match steady as she waited for the fire to burn steadily on the head. "I kept asking Ahyi, and each time she'd ask me to do something, like help with grinding the corn." Xinying dropped the match next to the dried twigs.

"But that grinding machine makes so much noise."

"Exactly! It swallowed up all my questions," Xinying said. "She tried everything to avoid answering."

Kai followed her gaze to the little flame, then looked at her again. Her mouth had turned downward.

"I gave up asking. Then one day, Ahyi finally told me. Ma had gone to join Pa in the city to work. I haven't seen them since. They send money when they can."

"Pa doesn't always send money either. He saves up and sends it to us every few months. It costs less that way. But once, when he was living in the dormitory, all his money was stolen."

"That's terrible! Factories are horrible places. When Ma started her job, her new employer kept her pay for six months."

"Why did they do that?"

"To stop her from quitting. If she left, she lost the money."

The flame looked like it was dying, so Kai got on his knees and threw in some dried leaves. He fanned the fire with his hand. "So they left you with your Uncle and Auntie Liang."

"Yes, and now Ahyi's away too." Xinying threw in more dead leaves. "She's gone to the factory to work, after Uncle had his accident."

Kai stopped fanning. "Uncle Liang had an accident?"

"He's alright now, but when he first went to work they didn't teach him how to use the machine properly." She covered the tips of her left hand fingers with her right hand. "So now all his fingers on his left hand are the same."

"So now all his fingers are all the same size?" Kai tore his eyes away from the fire to look at Xinying. "His fingers got chopped off?"

"Only three of them. The little one was short anyway." She wriggled her little finger. "So the blade missed it."

"Pa never talks about his work." Kai turned back to make sure the little flame was burning on its own now. He sat down again and crossed his legs. "Whenever he would call us, he would say he was working very hard, and he would tell me to study hard. That he's gone away to work for me."

"So, that they can pay for our school fees and uniforms."

"And clothes and food." Kai tucked his chin between his knees.

The dried twigs suddenly burst into huge flames. Xinying sat on her ankles and straightened her body. "That's why we have to study very hard." The color had flowed to her face like she was bursting. "So that one day we'll be able to get a job that pays lots of money, and our parents won't ever have to leave us." She became silent and watched the fire dance for a minute. "Then they can be around to nag and scold us." She threw him a crooked smile. "I know it sounds stupid, but if my ma were here to do that, it'd be music to me." Kai stayed silent. "Of course, I miss the nice things too, like her cooking or even everyday things, like tying up my hair."

He knew what she meant. Living with Yee Por was not as bad

as he had thought. Although she wasn't as mobile, she watched him closely as he did the various chores. Even if he didn't know how to do something, she never lost her patience. For example, she taught him how to cook new dishes; what sauces to use and when to add them. Yee Por always asked about school and if he was happy, and listened to his complaints too. But she wasn't Ma. He took out the drawing from his pocket. Since the incident with the bullies, he had kept it in his pocket with the marble. It was already ruined with wrinkles, so a few more fold lines did not matter. At least it was safe in his pocket. He unfolded it, remembering the sequence of how the picture was drawn.

"Did you draw that with your ma? You're so lucky." She went quiet for a while. The water began to boil. "Come on, let's go back now. I've got to sweep the floor."

"It's the fifth day tomorrow." Kai reminded her. "The first part finishes tomorrow."

"Then we must bring our shovels for the next part."

Like the days before, they set off for home together, with Kai sloshing water as he stepped over big rocks and Xinying dodging branches at eye level. The next day, Kai took Lee's shovel with him when he went to the river. Xinying took her uncle's spade. But things did not go according to plan.

Chapter 19

Traffic crawled on the highway. Lee looked in his mirror. There was more action in the back than on the road. Da Laopan had unbuckled his seatbelt and spread his papers on the back seat. He glanced between two sheets, put one down, and picked up another. Backward and forward with those papers.

For the umpteenth time, Lee rolled the car forward when the lorry in front moved. But this time, the lorry chugged further. The distance between them increased. Lee stepped on his accelerator and closed the gap between them again. Red lights flashed up. Lee jammed his brakes. Laopan jolted. He put his hand out in front of him, just in time to stop his head from banging on the driver's seat. The papers in his hand were crushed.

"Sorry," Lee said. The truck in front moved again. He released his brakes. "The jam's clearing, or at least we're coming up to the junction. Probably everyone's getting off this highway."

"Is that our junction?" Da Laopan took off his glasses.

"Yes, we're nearly at the warehouse now. You can just see the back of it." Lee gave a quick nod in the northwest direction.

"Oh, yes, I see where we are now. Do you know what's happening at the back?" Da Laopan asked, referring to the back section of the warehouse.

"It's coming along really well, sir. The men are working in the evenings and weekends. They've done the partitioning and the doors. The plumbing for the toilets is being installed at the moment."

"When do you think it'll be ready?" Laopan leaned back on his leather seat.

"We're aiming to have it ready for the new school year." Lee indicated left.

"Good, good."

Lee was not sure whether Da Laopan was pleased about leaving the standstill traffic or about the progress of the childcare center. Nevertheless, this was a good moment. Laopan's generosity meant his family could be together. It was a privilege for workers of certain rank. Lee qualified, being right at the bottom of the cutoff grade. He knew he was fortunate. "Yes, everyone I've spoken to is looking forward to it, to bring their children here. Some of them have not seen them for years." But as soon as the words came out, the air in the car felt thicker than the haze outside. So Lee concentrated on the road ahead, not daring to look at his employer. If he had dared to peek at his rear mirror at that moment, he would have seen Da Laopan's contorted face.

Da Laopan could still remember that day vividly.

He and Mrs. Laopan were enjoying their cheong fun, made more delicious because the grandson on his lap was slurping up every spoonful of the white noodle rolls. His late son's wife was also at the breakfast table.

"There is something I need to tell you." Her voice quivered.

They both looked up. What was she up to this time?

"You've been very kind to me and Ah Fu. You've let us stay on even after…" She stopped, opened her mouth, but no words came out. Then she tried again. Her voice box failed her again.

Mrs. Laopan tutted.

It was the catalyst she needed. The words came rushing out like spilled tea. "You know I loved your son, but he is gone. I met someone a while back, and he's being posted overseas. He's asked me to go with him. I hope you will give me your blessings."

They'd had good fortune until she came along. She must have offended the spirits. How else could she have given them a grandson but lost her husband afterward? A new life given, but another life taken. Ah Fu was exchanged for their son, their only son, the one to pass on the family name. Now she wanted to leave. Da Laopan knew exactly how to respond.

"You have been a respectful daughter-in-law, but the heavens have been cruel. You're still young and pretty. We will not hold you to this family. Go. Go and marry this man."

"Thank you, thank you for being understanding!" She came toward him to take Ah Fu.

Immediately, he put his arms round the boy. "But you must go alone, Ah Fu stays with us."

"You can't do that!"

"His surname is Yang. He belongs to this family."

"But he's my son!"

"And you'll have plenty more. You're still young. Start a family with your new man. Forget about Ah Fu. He's ours. He belongs here."

"Please!" Her face twisted.

"You are not taking him away from this family. We've already lost a son. You'll have to make a choice."

She tried to take Ah Fu off him, but he was stronger. There was a lot of crying and shouting, and Ah Fu was tugged backward and forward. In the end, Da Laopan ordered the servants to throw her out of the mansion. The boy never saw his mother again.

Da Laopan and Mrs. Laopan made up for her absence. They gave Ah Fu everything; delicious food, soft clothing, warm lodgings, and a houseful of toys. All the things a child could ever want. He grew up thoroughly spoilt. He'd throw tantrums if things were not fetched for him. At first, Da Laopan thought they had overindulged Ah Fu and they reigned in their excesses. But the boy only got worse. That was when they noticed his body was not growing normally.

It must be punishment. Retribution.

Maybe, Da Laopan had thought, if he performed good deeds he might earn the forgiveness of the Heavens and good fortune would come back to his life. But how could he make up for separating a child from his mother?

He knew hundreds of his factory workers depended on him. Many of them had to leave their own children behind to work for him. Like Lee. Now Mei too. She left her son behind for this job, but what if the temple man was right about Ah Fu's health? He shuddered at that thought.

No, he couldn't be too late to make up for his sins. The childcare service in his factory was nearly ready. No child of his employees would be separated from their parents again. Other factory owners thought he was an old fool to squander his money like that, but his own workers were now his family. Like Ah Sau.

When she first arrived, Ah Sau was a young widow with a toddler in tow. His business was in its humble beginnings. Now, his company prospered, and Han towered over everyone. A big commerce needed people he could trust. Han grew up in his employment and he brought in other people he trusted. Da Laopan did not get out. He gave his scalp a distracted scratch.

"Have you heard from Han since he left?"

"No." Lee loosened his seatbelt to turn around.

"Neither have I. He's not answered any of my calls." The old man rubbed his eyes like a tired baby. "I didn't think it through properly," he said. "All I cared for was Ah Fu." Da Laopan opened his palms like he was going to claw himself. "Sending Han into the mountains to prepare it, when he didn't know the area. And the treatment didn't even make any sense, boil and cool overnight five times."

He slumped back against the soft seat. The furrow between his eyebrows was as deep as the Big River.

"Lee, please go and fetch Han back."

"Yes." Lee made the reply he always did to any of Laopan's demands. Then the meaning of the request hit him. "Of course!"

"You know the way, so as least I know you won't get lost. I really should have sent you in the first place."

Laopan's handphone rang. "What's wrong?" Laopan did not stand on ceremony with only one person. "Is it Ah Fu?"

When Laopan hung up, he said, "Lee, go now. Tell Han to come home with whatever he's prepared so far."

Chapter 20

The sun had long passed its highest point when Lee arrived at the hamlet. He would have made his way through the rocky path in the morning sun, but the bus had broken down.

Lee always knew there was no future in these mountains. Word had gone around about well-paying jobs in the factories. Without hesitation, he had left for the city. He had started out as one of the hundreds in a factory making sugar from sugar cane. After the long hours and only one day off a month, he collected his wages and invested them in lessons to better himself. This meant he did not have much money to send home, but he knew he was investing for their future. The city was developing, unlike the countryside. Nothing here had changed since the day he left.

Coming back so soon after the New Year celebrations, he felt like an outsider, like the stranger his son had become to him. About the only thing he knew about Kai was his love for animals. So he made sure he returned with a new piglet for him every year. He spent any spare cash on presents, such as clothes and household wares. After all, having these luxuries was the reason he went away. He always bought a bag of dried millet, for emergencies, in case of a bad year. Farming was never reliable.

Mei had never asked for any money since he left, until that telephone call. Harvest was never good enough in this mountain soil, but it was the only time he knew she had used the dried millet in desperation.

The time had come. Something had to be done.

He had been fortunate to stumble upon the coveted ahma position for Mei. However hard it was for mother and son, leaving Kai with Yee Por was the right thing to do.

Kai should be back from school by now. Lee climbed up the ladder to Yee Por's hut. "Yee Por! Kai! It's me!"

In her usual stoop, Yee Por had firewood in one arm. The other arm held on to a supporting strut. His eyes followed her trembling legs and the bandage. Lee leapt up the last step into the room.

"Yee Por, let me do it." Lee took the wood from her and strode over to the dying fire.

"Why are you here?"

"Where's Kai?" Lee asked, almost at the same time. "Nothing's wrong, Yee Por." Lee fanned the fire. "I was just sent here to bring Han back. We lost touch with him and couldn't get through on Liang's telephone."

"No, the telegraph poles are still down. Han was here, but he left after only one night. He should have been back by now. You must have just missed him when you left."

Lee glanced at Yee Por and turned his eyes back to the fire. His mind churned. Yee Por only knew of the slowest and cheapest bus to the city, but Laopan had paid for the fastest trains. So Han should have been back even before Lee had left. Something had happened. But there was no way of alerting Laopan if Liang's phone was down, and Lee did not have a handphone. He was not senior enough to be given one. He glanced at his watch. The last bus had already left. He would have to stay here overnight as planned.

"You may be a city man now, but you've not lost the skill to keep the fire going." Yee Por interrupted his thoughts.

Lee became aware of the fire's steady flicker and gave her a small smile. There was no need to say anything to Yee Por. It would only worry the old lady, who already had a bad leg to worry about. He looked about him. Kai's school bag dangled on the back of the wooden chair. "Where's Kai?"

"Gone to the river to get water. Probably Xinying's there with him too. They're always together after school."

Lee raised his eyebrows again.

"With the pig."

"That sounds more like Kai." Lee got to his feet. "I'll go and find him."

He told himself that no matter how Kai behaved, he would not lose his patience with him this time. He had promised Mei.

"You've been away for so long, you don't know your son at all. Try and be his friend. Don't talk down to him," she had said. "You'll see a different side to him."

He was skeptical.

"Do it for me, please?"

He knew how she would have loved to be sent here, but Ah Fu needed her constant care. For Mei's sake, he wanted to make full use of this bonus time with his son.

A distant, high-pitched voice attracted his attention. He peered over the edge of the rise. Below, a little figure staggered away from the river. Next to him, a black piglet scurried.

Both Kai and Pig looked bigger than he remembered. Kai stopped in his tracks and stared up in Lee's direction. Then he tottered forward again, his ungainly movements became even more exaggerated.

"Stay there!" Lee hurried down the rocky slope, keeping his eyes on his son, who had dropped the two water-filled buckets and gaped up at him. He stopped a few paces from Kai. "You've grown taller!"

Before he could find any more words to say, Kai threw his arms around Lee's waist, squeezing him tight. Lee nearly fell over, but he didn't mind. This must be what Mei was talking about; the side of Kai he never knew. Usually Kai greeted him with a fearful nod and a soft, "Pa, you're home" welcome.

His skin tingled. The next minute, a cold and wet snout sniffed his ankles.

"Pig, stop it. That's ticklish!" Kai broke away, giggling. His laughter echoed throughout the forest.

"He's grown quite a bit." Lee squatted down and rubbed his fingers between Pig's ears. In return, Pig waved his floppy ears forward and backward.

He felt arms round his neck again. "You're back! Is Ma back too?"

Lee tried to loosen the grip so he could breathe. He saw the gold chain at the base of Kai's neck. Mei would be pleased. "Ma's not here. She couldn't come. She had to look after the boy." The arms around him went limp. "He's really not well, needs a lot of looking after." Lee got up and waved at Xinying.

On cue, Xinying ran over with their empty baskets. He made a note to mention this to Mei. She would be pleased Kai had made a friend. He was also heartened with this development and did not notice the children were passing unspoken messages with their eyes about postponing their task as Lee's return was more important.

Lee adjusted the straps on Kai's basket so he could thread his arms through. "Come, let me show you what I've brought back for you." He put the bucket of water in Xinying's back-basket. "Or I should say, your ma wanted me to bring back for you." He slung Kai's basket on his own back and squatted down.

Kai hoisted the bucket into Lee's basket. "Ma's got more presents for me? Is it another marble?"

Back at Yee Por's hut, Lee opened his bag. "We bought you things that we thought you might need." He reached in and fished out the items one by one. "Exercise books, pens, pencils, an eraser, a ruler." Then he brought out a big pile of items. "We thought you might have outgrown your clothes, so here are some shirts and trousers, and here's a pair of shoes as well. If they're too big now, you'll soon grow into them."

"Wah! So many new things." Kai's head was emerging from the green T-shirt. Without waiting for his arms to come through the sleeves, he stuck his feet into the new shoes.

"Yes, with Ma working too, we can afford to buy a few more things." It was so delightful to see Kai with his presents. Lee wished Mei was here with him. "And I stopped on the way and bought all these." Lee held out the bags of fresh food. "I'll treat you to my cooking tonight."

"You can cook?"

"Of course! But not as well as Ma, or Yee Por!"

Yee Por was sitting on her chair. Her eyes had disappeared among the lines on her face.

Where usually a simple bowl of corn porridge, preserved pork, and chewy black fungus signified dinner, Lee served up fragrant rice, two meat dishes, vegetables, and even tofu soup.

"Just listen," Lee said.

Kai cocked his ears and frowned. "I can't hear anything."

"Except the cackling fire," Yee Por said.

"That's right," Lee said. "One of the things I really miss when I go back to the city," Lee picked out the fattest vegetable stem for Yee Por. "It's so quiet here."

"What about Ma? What does she miss?" Kai skimmed the top of the bowl with his spoon, where the soup was coolest.

"Well, that's easy. You, of course." Lee helped himself to the fried garlic slices. "She's always talking about you, like the way you blow too hard on your soup."

Instantly Kai stopped blowing and grinned at Lee.

Lee continued. "The way you tumble with Pig. The way you put the basket on your back. The way you do everything!"

Kai bent down to slurp his soup, so Lee did not see his shining eyes.

"She wonders what you're doing. If you're managing school work and if you are helping Yee Por." Lee added another spoonful of soup into Yee Por's bowl.

"I couldn't have done it without Kai, especially with this useless leg." Yee Por picked out the juiciest pork onto Kai's bowl. "Kai's looked after me, doing everything—washing, cooking, and planting."

"That's a good boy, guai!" Lee said. "You're doing your bit for your family," he started. He had just praised Kai. Usually he only had criticism for everything Kai did. Did Mei's absence improve Kai's behavior, or was it because he had seen it from Mei's point of view?

Even Kai looked uncomfortable.

Yee Por broke the awkward silence. "If not for him collecting water every day, we wouldn't have enough even to drink."

"Yes, when I found them, Kai was carrying the buckets," Lee said gratefully. He forced himself to come up with something Mei would say if she were here. "Tell me about the game you were playing with Xinying. Why was there a big pot? What were those brown nuts on the ground?"

Chapter 21

"We were about to bury them when you arrived." Kai concluded his tale of Han and the fruit treatment. "How long will you be staying?"

"I'm definitely staying here tonight." Lee tried to sound relaxed, but his thoughts still lingered on Kai's story. "Do you want to come back to our house tonight?"

Lee left the hearth burning with a slow fire, with the familiar cooking pot resting on top. The sky above was just turning orange to greet the sun. In the distance, a bird chirped and another replied. He climbed down and surveyed the house, checking that every stilt was sturdy and every panel solid. Kai finally appeared at the doorway.

"Ah, you're awake," Lee said. "Let's have something to eat and then we'll go to the river."

At the river bank, Han's pot sat among the scattered shells from the previous day. Lee knelt by the mound and released his basket. He reached for his shovel and pressed it into the ground. The shovel slid in.

"Pa, what are you doing?" Kai knelt down beside Lee.

"This is the next step, isn't it?" Lee scooped soil into the pot. "If I carry it back like this, covered in the soil-ash, it will have been buried for at least a day by the time I return. This'll save us time." He carried on without looking up, so he did not see the color drain from Kai's face. "We could give some of it to the little master. If he recovers, great. If not, we'll keep the rest in the soil until the time is ripe." He paused, rested his right hand on the ground and looked up at Kai. "Either way, we'll have it with us at the mansion."

"No, don't take mine." Kai covered the mouth of the pot with his arms and leaned over it. "I might not have done it right. I didn't do the same as Uncle Han, remember?"

"But you followed the temple's instructions, and Laopan wants me to bring it back now. We're running out of time, and the fire fruit is our last hope."

"Why don't you just let him DIE?" Kai shouted so loud the rocks on the mountains repeated after him, "Die! Die! Die!"

"Choy!" Lee roared back. He had expected Kai to know it was bad to wish death upon anyone.

Kai hung his head.

Silently, Lee chided himself for losing his patience yet again.

"I just want Ma to come home."

Lee put the shovel down. "I know this is hard on you, but you must understand. Ma won't be coming back here. We can't rely on farming. You saw how bad it got last year." Lee put his hands on Kai's bony shoulders. "If Ah Fu dies and Ma loses her job, she will find work elsewhere, like in the factories. It'll be hard for her. Long tiring hours, sweaty and crowded dormitories. She'll be among hundreds of other workers. Nobody will look out for her." Lee shuddered. "I've done that for too many years." He let out a deep breath. "But you know what? That's still better than starving here. If you really love Ma, then you, we, should do whatever we can, for her sake, to save the young master. Help her keep her ahma job."

With his head down, Kai handed back the pot. Lee gave him a proud pat. He never suspected Kai was thinking about Uncle Liang's horrific experience in a factory. Without speaking, they buried the seeds with the soil and ash until the pot was full.

"We'll keep the rest here." Lee looked at his watch. "I have to catch the last bus. I won't have time to walk you back to the house."

He stood up.

"You're not saying goodbye to Yee Por?" Kai avoided eye contact.

"I've already said goodbye to her. You were still asleep." Lee knelt down and clutched Kai's upper arms.

Kai threw himself at Lee. His body sag against him, face buried in his collarbone. "I hope the young master gets better." Lee did not see how Kai squeezed his eyes to stop any tears from escaping.

"You're doing your part for our family, just like I've got to go and do my part now." Lee shifted Kai backward so he could look at his son one more time. "You look after yourself."

The sun shot arrows through the trees. The gold chain on Kai's neck gleamed.

Lee pointed to the pendant underneath Kai's shirt. "Ma will be pleased it's looking after you!"

Little did Lee anticipate that the next time he saw this pendant it would be on a dead body.

Chapter 22

The fresh mound of soil and ash smelled more bitter than the yellow rapeseed in bloom.

Pa had never returned home mid-year before. He only came back because he was sent, and then he had rushed back because of his boss' grandson. Work was more important, not Kai. That cut his heart. What he said about Ma was even more painful. She would never come back here. He used to think Ma was the only person who cared about him. But she had decided to go away, and stay away.

But he brought presents. Lots of wonderful presents, a little voice in him argued. *That showed they cared. They were thinking of you.*

"I'd rather have nothing!"

The mountain rocks echoed back "Have nothing! Have nothing!"

"And have Ma here with me again," he whispered. This time, he did not worry about tears spilling from his eyes.

"Kai?" a musical voice called out.

Quickly, Kai dried his face, but he did not answer. He just wanted to drag his feet back to the hut and bury himself under the blanket for the rest of the day. A little black pig scurried out from the bushes, trying hard to run away from the rope he was tied to. Behind him a pair of orange trainers appeared.

"Yee Por told me you were at your place, so I went over," Xinying handed the rope to Kai. "Pig was squealing like a fire cracker. There he was, with one trotter stuck in the struts, trying to escape."

Kai looked at the wrinkled face of his black piglet. "You were trying to find me?" He scratched the space between his ears. "No, I haven't abandoned you," Kai said bitterly.

"Your pa left?"

"Yes." Kai hands stopped for a minute. "And he took some of our fruit."

Pig's floppy ears flicked forward and dropped back. He seemed to understand what Kai had said. He whined like he was relating a sorrowful story and sniffed Kai's ankles, as if not believing they had been reunited. Kai rubbed his back, and at once Pig turned over.

"He's so cute," Xinying said. "He wants you to rub his belly."

A small part of him had expected her to say something nice about being abandoned by his father. But she was only interested in Pig. Kai leaned forward and gave his charge a little rub. Pig lay there almost motionless. When he stopped, the piglet waved his trotters.

"What happens if you stop stroking him?" Xinying asked.

As if he had understood Xinying's question, Pig shifted his position and sat on Kai's left foot. He twisted his body around and gazed at Kai with his soulful eyes. Kai stroked him. For a while, he said nothing. At least Pig wanted him.

"Do you want to finish the last step?" Xinying asked, her voice gentle.

Over the past five days, they had emptied the water on the same spot, so the ground parted easily, as Lee had discovered earlier. Whilst Kai and Xinying dug, Pig dug too. His white trotters were soon camouflaged. Without warning, the ground from underneath gave way, and Pig rolled right in. Each time he tried to clamber up, the wall collapsed.

"Come on." Xinying squatted down. Beads of sweat had formed on her high forehead. "I'll grab one front leg and you grab the other."

"Don't worry, Pig. We'll pull you out." He managed to catch one of the front trotters. "I've got you."

But Pig struggled to balance on his hindlegs while trying to scale the wall. They stayed like this, scrambling and tugging, but never coordinated. Then all of a sudden, one big push with his hindlegs timed with one big heave from Kai and Xinying, and a muddy Pig rocketed out.

Pig landed next to Kai. He got up. Kai jumped away and ran

for his bucket. Pig followed his master. Kai lifted his bucket and looked at Pig, who turned and ran toward Xinying, but not before the water landed on his back. Brown dripped off the black body, revealing streaks of white trotters.

"Yes!" Kai punched the air. But Pig shook off the water and sprayed the muddy drops on him. "Aiyoh!" He tried to sound annoyed, but his eyes gave him away. Xinying was hysterical, unable to wrap the fruit in the big leaves.

Bolstered by Xinying's giggles, Kai carried on playing water chase with Pig. The initial coolness of the water soon became chilly as the sun lowered. His new shirt had almost dried. But a patch on his trousers remained damp. He put his hands on the wet patch.

"I'm so stupid." Kai pulled out a wet folded paper from his pocket. "Stupid! Stupid! Stupid!"

"Don't try to open it now, it's too wet," Xinying said. "You'll tear it."

"It's ruined! I'm so stupid."

"It's not ruined, only wet." She grabbed her empty basket. "Why don't you put it in here to air dry? It won't get blown away in here."

Kai dropped it in. He saw Xinying had already buried the fruit. It was just as well. A fresh mound of brown soil stood out against last winter's yellow twigs and new green sprouts.

Xinying gave the soil one final pat. "So, now we wait."

Chapter 23

Lee set off with a sense of urgency. The more he thought about it, the more he knew things were not right. There was no reason for Han to not have been back before Lee had left Laopan's residence.

The blue skies cleared the way for the sun to unleash its heat. Flies hummed and buzzed about. Some landed on him, and he brushed them off. They flew away and landed on him again, only on a different part of his body. Landing, chased off, landing, this flirting went on for a bit. Lee no longer brushed them away; he tried to smack them but thwacked himself instead. Every single time he missed. A cool breeze came, like ice on his overheated skin.

Lee filled his lungs with the freshness, but it was not as fresh as it should have been. He detected a strange whiff. Not an odor he had come across before. He looked about him. Apart from the incessant flies, his surroundings were as he expected—green leaves and stony ground. He halted. The leaves rustled and the birds chirped. No extraordinary sounds, no voices. Ignoring the flies, Lee kept a lookout for this abnormal scent. It came and went, depending on the direction of the breeze. The path continued downhill and twisted sharply around a big tree. He turned the corner and stopped in his tracks. Beyond the protruding rocks, there was the vague outline of a person. The sense of unease building in him compelled Lee forward. The clothes looked familiar.

"Hello?"

No response. He called again, a little louder this time. He edged forward. Through the forest path, he could see flies were swarming now. The whiff intensified to a smell that wrenched his stomach. The person lying face down stayed on the ground.

He held his breath and tapped the outstretched arm. The body was cold. He lifted its shoulder and drew his breath sharply. It might have been the shock of what he saw or the deep inhaling of the stench around him. Lee's stomach lurched, and its contents emptied out.

Han looked like he was asleep.

Despite the stench and the swarming flies, Lee shook Han. His body moved without any resistance and then lay limp. Lee pulled his collar over his nose and looked around. There was no evidence of blood on Han and no bruise marks. Next to him was a pot exactly like the one he was carrying. Inside were the same ovoid-shaped seeds soaking in water, except for one on the ground not far from Han's outstretched arm. It had been cracked opened.

Chapter 24

I n the days after Lee's departure, the weather was unusually warm
and dry for spring. As Yee Por's ankle was slow to mend, the
responsibility fell on Kai to collect firewood after school on top
of the daily water trips. That meant less time for homework and
more time outdoors with Pig. He often imagined he was on one of
his trips to the river with Mei. He had not heard from his parents
since Lee's departure. Even if they had tried, they couldn't have
called. The telegraph poles were still down. As he broke off dead
branches, he wondered if the young master was still alive and if Mei
was still the ahma. Over the week, Kai made a huge stockpile of
wood indoors in preparation for the overdue spring deluge.

Ever since the accident, Yee Por could only potter about in the
house while Kai was at school. On market days like today, she had

only the company of Pig's occasional squeal. Her movements were so slow, it took her almost a full day to light the oil lamps and burn offerings for the Gods. She needed many sit-downs in between, but she always had the cooking fire lit for Kai when he got back.

On this day, like she had done several times over, Yee Por lifted the wooden hearth cover and lit the fire. She left the fire dancing and hobbled over to the side to fetch the cooking pot.

In the distance, Pig was busy by the bamboo fence. He dug away soil until there was a gap under the struts. Then he pushed his head forward. At first, his snout couldn't fit. He dug some more and pushed his head again. Before long, the hole was big enough for his snout. He carried on with this game—digging, testing, and digging again.

At this moment, when Yee Por left the fire to dance, Pig succeeded in squeezing his head through, except the hole was not big enough for his body. When he discovered he could neither go forward nor back into the pen, he squealed for Kai.

Pig's painful and urgent squeal made Yee Por jump. She landed on her bad ankle, crumpled over, and hit her head against the praying altar on the way down. Her head exploded in pain. She landed with her good leg protruding at an awkward angle through her hips. The last thing she remembered, was a warm wetness coming down her face and a searing pain below her waist. She was not aware that the altar had also fallen over onto the pile of dry firewood, scattering it. The wood by the burning embers caught alight. Before long, Yee Por's house was ablaze.

White paper banners with words and pictures in black ink adorned the hamlet. Heart wrenching howls expelled from the villagers' lungs. Each time a gust of wind blew, they made flapping noises applauding the life of Yee Por.

Kai did not remember much of Yee Por's funeral, except that Xinying sat with him throughout and spoke for him each time someone came up to say a kind word. All he could do was ogle at the enormous chest in which they had put Yee Por, the chest Yee Por called her longevity chest. Ironically, it was not damaged in the fire.

He also remembered when Uncle Liang came up to them.

"Kai, come quickly. Your parents are on the phone."

The telephone had finally been reconnected on the day of Yee Por's accident, but the connection had been intermittent. So Kai ran. He ran as fast as that day when he pulled Pig out from the fence and then saw that the black smoke rising through the trees was in fact coming from Yee Por's house. The memory of that day, the guilt, the shock, all came to the fore the minute he heard Mei's voice. In the end, Uncle Liang pried the receiver from a sobbing Kai.

After the funeral, Kai headed up the mountain. Staring at what used to be his home, this lone hut was his abode again. It was the obvious solution. He had been bunking at Uncle Liang's since the blaze, but Yee Por had been laid to rest now. Her hut was unlivable. Uncle Liang's had only been a temporary sanctuary.

Kai felt for the marble in his pocket. When he was feeling rough, its smoothness comforted him. His little finger brushed against paper. It was crispy now. After it had dried out, Xinying showed him how to pry it open. She did it without tearing even one bit, which was miraculous given the condition it was in before the accident. It was frayed at the fold lines. Some parts were so bad, holes had appeared, so he stole some sticky tape from school to mend them.

He had drawn himself running toward the hut. Their hut. Yee Por was here when Mei and Lee first left him. Now even Yee Por had left him. He went into the enclosure. A little pink snout came charging toward him. Kai bent over to scratch his forehead, but Pig went in circles around his legs with his straight tail wagging.

Kai sat down. Pig clambered onto his lap and lay on his back. For the first time since the fire, Kai felt warm. He was not alone. "You want your belly rubbed?" Pig answered him by lying still. "I guess you'll be happy now that I'm living upstairs again."

Kai sat with Pig like that. He watched the bliss in Pig's eyes as he stroked. With each stroke, Pig remained transfixed. With every stroke, Kai felt warmer.

A shadow made Kai look up.

Chapter 25

He recognized the silhouette of Uncle Liang standing at the gate.

"I've confirmed it with your parents. You're staying with me from now onward."

Kai stared at Uncle Liang. Thoughts and emotions fluttered like the joss paper at Yee Por's funeral.

Moving again. Moving from home to Yee Por's and now to Uncle Liang's. Never belonging anywhere.

I won't be living alone. I'll have Xinying for company.

Xinying is a good friend, but why would Uncle Liang want me? There are already too many people in his house.

Pig nuzzled his snout on Kai. Kai looked down at the little black bundle. Pig licked his arm. At least he knew for sure Pig wanted him. Why deceive himself that anyone else really wanted him? He would be better off living on his own.

Kai shook his head. "I'll be fine. I'll just stay here." He pointed to Pig. "I've got to look after him."

"But you can still come and see him every day, like you've been doing."

Kai shook his head again. "He tried to escape. If I hadn't stopped to rescue him, I…"

Uncle Liang opened the gate and stepped in. "You were at school, Kai."

Yes, but I could have discovered the fire sooner, Kai wanted to say, except it was too painful to hear the words out loud.

"I could've been back from the market sooner, or our neighbors could've come back from the fields sooner." Uncle Liang squatted down next to him. Pig scuttled off.

Pig was fascinating, the way his body wobbled when he scratched his back against the fence.

"We were all out for the day, Kai, not just you."

Whatever consoling words Uncle Liang said, it would not change anything.

"We'll all miss her. You don't have to do this on your own."

Kai squeezed his eyes tight. He must not let Uncle Liang, or anyone, witness another embarrassing debacle again. He made up his mind. "I can't. Pig misses me."

"But it doesn't mean you have to live here on your own."

Kai looked at Uncle Liang straight in the eye. "Because I wasn't living upstairs, he got lonely and tried to find me." *I've lost Yee Por, and I nearly lost Pig*, he thought.

"Yee Por would not like this. And besides, I have promised your parents." Uncle Liang's voice was firm, and he stood up as if the conversation was over. Except he then crumbled over and winced. "Oh, my leg's got pins and needles again."

Kai could not help smirking. Uncle Liang was a muscular man, but at that moment his leg bones seemed to have dissolved. "I'll walk to school with Xinying every day. Yee Por would like that."

That smirk, or maybe his words, had an effect.

"I suppose we can try this for now," Uncle Liang said eventually. "But just remember," he put his hand on Kai's shoulder, "you're one of us. There'll always be plenty of room for you."

To Uncle Liang, Kai simply nodded. It was easier not to say anything. But he had made a promise to Pig to look after him always. Look what happened when he broke that promise and went to live with Yee Por. Pig had tried to escape at least twice. No, he would have to lose Pig before he would move in with Uncle Liang.

Uncle Liang got up to leave. As he reached the gate, he stopped for a moment. Kai waited for him to open the gate. Instead, he turned around.

"Your Pa just told me," Uncle Liang ambled toward Kai again. "The fruit Han was treating," he paused, "they're no longer interested in it."

"Why?"

"They've changed their minds. Your pa doesn't want you to play with it anymore."

"We've not been doing anything with it. It's just buried in the ground."

"Good. Just leave it in the ground then."

"What happened?"

"Um…I don't know the details, except it makes you ill." Uncle Liang could have told him the truth about Han, but with Yee Por's death, this was not a good time.

Uncle Liang looked straight into Kai's eyes. "Don't go back to it anymore. It didn't work. It really isn't edible. Promise me."

When the moon began its ascent, Kai regretted his decision. He was sure Uncle Liang and Xinying would welcome him, but what if Wen and Chuan blabbed at school that he had appeared at theirs this late in the night? He could just see the rumors flying about. Kai was afraid of being alone. Kai was afraid of the dark. What a coward.

No, it would be better to stay put in this big, empty house. He had been sure they would come back when it was darker and talk him into staying with them. He lay on the rug and stared at the ceiling.

Without Ma or Yee Por, the walls seemed to recoil away from his pitiful little being. Kai put Ma's pendant to his lips. He shivered. It was cold, like the world he was living in. He remembered when

Ma would settle him on the rug on those wonderful nights with her adoring eyes and her warm smile. She was the kindest and gentlest mother anyone could have. Ma always stroked his back and sang her favorite song. He turned over on his stomach, pretending she was next to him like always. Even though the house was devoid of human sounds, he could almost hear her silvery voice vibrating to the last line of the first verse.

It was as if she would cast a spell with that line. He never managed to stay awake after the first verse. The instant he turned over, Kai fell asleep on the threadbare rug.

When he opened his eyes, he knew it was still early, so he scrutinized the faded fibers on the rug. He had spent the night on his own. Uncle Liang and Xinying did not come to coax him back to their hut. It only showed they did not want him in their house.

Nobody wanted him.

"I'll meet you here after school. We can collect water together," Xinying said when she came for him. Her black hair was tied in a ponytail today.

"No need." The words rushed out of him. Xinying looked hurt. *Hypocrite, you didn't come for me last night.* Yet he searched for a reason to soften his rude reply. He squeezed the paper in his pocket. "I know you're busy. You've got to revise for those big tests."

"Yes, I suppose." Xinying pursed one side of her lips. "Uncle has to sort out Yee Por's hut, so I've got to do all the other chores too."

"Can we go to Yee Por's house?" Wen asked.

"No, you've got to stay with me. Uncle will have chores for you to do."

"What does he want us to do?" Chuan asked.

"Our part for the family, of course," Wen said. "Haven't you been paying attention in class?"

"Of course I have! But what exactly?" Chuan said.

Kai stopped listening, partly because when Wen or Chuan started, it went round and round in circles. But mainly because Wen's words reminded him of what Lee always lectured.

Do your part for your family.

He crushed Mei's drawing in his pocket. What exactly were they doing for him by leaving him behind? If there were a fire nearby, he would fling the drawing straight into the flames. He walked to school hardly speaking. He spoke to no one at school and walked back in silence.

From that day on, he spoke enough to keep Xinying at bay. The little house was empty of happy sounds, only the solemn grinding of farming and chores. Some days he consoled himself with a humble harvest. The yellow leaves meant that the tubers were ready, and he dug them out. But they were very hard. With all his might, he was just able to peel the skin and cut them up without cutting himself. By the time he had finished, he barely had the energy to cook them.

The clouds covering the mountain peaks could not sit as low

as his spirits. He no longer tried at school, especially not when they were teaching irrelevant topics like moral education—country and family above all. How was that relevant to him with his absent parents whom the teacher could not summon to talk to about his bad grades? Often he did not feel like doing his usual chores, even collecting water or firewood. He could not see the point of it all.

Except Pig was always there. When he squealed, he reminded Kai to look inside the enclosure. He did not notice it happened only on the weekend. Usually Pig wanted something. His water trough was empty or food basin was bare or the waste pile was spreading out too far across the enclosure. He came to the conclusion that Pig needed him in the same way he wanted Ma around. So for Pig's sake, he carried out his duties. Unlike ma and pa, he was not going to fall short on Pig.

By and by, the drudgery wore him down, like the slow and constant dripping of rainwater on the rock under the corner of his roof, until a hollow formed in the middle.

Chapter 26

"Hey!" Xinying's shrill voice rang through the deserted hills. He had seen her climbing up the path, but pretended he was not aware of her approach. "Are you avoiding me?"

Kai shrugged and continued to mix the fertilizer with the soil. Xinying watched him, like she was waiting for an explanation.

"What do you mean?" He forced out the lie. "We walk to school together every day."

"Yes, but that's not the same." She twirled her finger round a straggly leaf. "You don't say much, not like when we used to chat by the river."

Kai shrugged again and bent his head back toward the plants. He tried to stay disillusioned, but something inside him lifted. He was missed. "Who can get their words in edgeways when Wen and

Chuan are around?"

"That's mean." She gave his upper arm a little punch.

"It's true." He attempted to look serious when he turned toward Xinying, who pretended to look annoyed. Then she snorted, which made Kai snort, and they ended up laughing at each other for laughing over nothing.

She wiped her eyes on her sleeves. "Hey, I've been counting the days." The excitement in her voice made him look up. He tried hard not to smile, but it was infectious. It wasn't really her fault his life was so wretched. "The final day's on the eve of the Dumpling Festival. No school the next day, isn't that great?

"And when school reopens there's that assembly about Qu Yuan. A patriot, his sacrifice, the river dragon would eat his body, so people made dumplings to throw in the river, blah, blah, blah."

"I've had two more years of that than you."

"Why do they have to do it every year?"

"Actually, I don't mind it this year. Seniors give the talk and I want to do something different this year. Like you said, it's so boring to hear it year after year. So, I've had an idea. You know Qu Yuan is the true bit, but the dragon is the myth. Well, this dumpling tradition has been passed down the generations. History and myth merged to form tradition."

"And?"

"I know Uncle said it's not edible, but the fire fruit is sort of like that. A fruit that holds the cure, but only after it's been boiled and buried. We'll bring them in and show them at assembly—the Secret of the Great Fire Tree. We'll bring one that's not been cooked and display it. We'll open the cooked shells and show the insides. Who knows, maybe the color's changed." She gasped. "Maybe it's changed dramatically! The fire's leaving its mark on the fruit, making it look disgusting, to put us off, because it's such a sacred tree, an old, ancient, sacred tree. Not to be desecrated by being eaten. But the wise know its hidden power. Its power to heal." She beamed at him when she finished.

Something was missing. Kai thought for a bit. "That's why the original fruit is poisonous, to put us off. The ancient creators never thought we would come up with a way to get rid of the poison, but we did, by five days of boiling and forty nights' burial."

It was a good story.

"Of course, I'll share the fact that you inspired this. You must take the credit."

His thoughts clouded. Attract attention to himself? That would be like leaving the crops open to feasting birds. He would be there for children to mock and jeer, for people to point and whisper; the boy who was left behind, was so lonely he resorted to making up stories about a useless tree.

"What's wrong?"

"Nothing." He turned back to the ground and parted the topsoil between two plants. He could not really say all of this to Xinying. "I just miss my Ma and Pa."

"Mmm," Xinying said.

Kai could feel her eyes as he spooned fertilizer into the hole. He covered it up. "I wish I didn't feel sad about them."

"That's not possible."

"But you don't."

"Says who?"

"You're always so happy."

"Hmph! Of course I feel sad. Who wouldn't feel sad? I've cried and cried. I've cried until my eyes were so swollen I wished they'd fall out. I've cried until my throat was sore. I've cried until no tears would come." She sat down heavily next to him. "But they still stayed away."

It was as if he had lifted the lid of a bubbling rice pot, all the steam rushed out at once. Xinying was quiet for a moment. She was as stunned as he with that outburst.

"Sorry, I didn't know."

She did not hear him. Lifting her right arm, she swiped her sleeve against her wet cheek. Then she did it again with her left arm. "But later, I learned something from Uncle, when he had his accident." Her voice was calmer.

"What's that?"

Kai waited while Xinying parted the soil with her fingers. "When the factory sent him home, he slept all the time. And when he was awake, he just stared into space or at the bandage over his left hand." She paused for a minute, looking around.

Kai passed her the bag of fertilizer.

"They stopped his salary straightaway, so Ahyi had to go out and work. She found a job in a factory assembling sport shoes. It's quite safe, but she has to work until nine or ten o'clock every night."

"So she wasn't around, just you and Uncle."

Xinying nodded. "It was horrible. He couldn't do anything with one hand in bandages. And he wouldn't talk to us. It was like this for a very long time."

"Awful."

"But after a while, he was his usual happy self again, doing the farming and carving his wood and singing like he was a popstar."

Kai chuckled. Uncle Liang did have a deep melodic voice. "What happened?"

"He said there was no point mourning over what was lost or what was past. Or else he would be reliving the horror of that accident for the rest of his life." Xinying covered up the hole with the fertilizer and looked at Kai. "He said we can all choose what we do, whether we wanted to let the setback really set us back." She patted the mound firmly. "I didn't like Uncle when he was down. Normal Uncle was much more fun, always joking and saying nice things and doing nice things and, you know, he really cares about you." Xinying's dimples were resolute. "So I decided I would be like him, and be happy for what I have."

"So that's your secret formula," Kai said.

The fertilizing job was complete. From his squatting position, he let his bottom drop to the ground and crossed his legs.

"I wish I could carve like him though."

The gold chain was irritating his skin, so Kai brushed his grubby hand against his trousers and lifted it out over his stained shirt. Xinying tilted her head to take a closer look. "That's really pretty. Did your ma give it to you?"

He looked down at the round jade, the precious heirloom dangling against his dirty white top. It must have looked an unbefitting backdrop for something so elegant. The day Ma clasped it around his neck was still fresh in his mind. He nodded.

"My ma would never trust me with something like that." Xinying rubbed her hands together. The soil fell. Hands clean, she lifted the pendant to feel it. "It's so smooth. Ma'd be afraid I'd lose it."

"You can't lose this one," Kai said.

"Why not? What if you drop it or someone steals it?"

He shook his head. "It's got special powers. It exacts revenge on anyone who steals it. Wherever it is, it will somehow find its way back into our hands again."

"Who told you that?"

"Ma told me. This was all my great-grandmother had when she ran away from the palace."

"The palace? Your great-grandmother was royalty?"

"There was trouble. They wanted to kill the Emperor and all the other people who lived there," Kai said. "Great-grandmother was one of them. So she ran away."

"And she came here?"

Kai nodded. "She figured it was so remote here that no one would find her. But she was still afraid. So afraid that she even burned all her papers, papers that told them who she really was, including the important papers that revealed she owned land." Kai knew Ma's version of the story almost word for word.

"You owned land?"

"Apparently, but she lost everything then." Kai let his fingers run over the character in the middle, remembering the number of times he had asked Ma to tell him the story. "But this pendant protected her. She survived the unrest and had her family around until she died. So I would say it's looked after her in times of danger and blessed her with family." He looked at Xinying, whose mouth was hanging open as if she was hungry for more. So he lowered his pitch and waved his arms as if he were a grand priest. "On behalf of the Heavenly Temples, I bestow this gift to you. This noble family has my eternal protection. Be warned, those who seek this, Pendant and nobility cannot be apart. If you separate them, pain and anguish will befall you!"

At that moment, his own words hit him.

"Wah, you should be in the opera," Xinying said.

For days after, Kai mulled over Xinying's account. He was no more pitiful than her. She whose mother slipped away while pretending to go to market, she who had to hold her foster family together when both uncle and auntie were absent. There was no resentment in her when she related that story, he noted with a pang of guilt.

One sentence kept coming back to his mind.

"We can all choose what we do, whether to let the setback really set us back."

Xinying was always happy because she made that choice.

The visit from Xinying rekindled a little fire inside Kai, allowing positive thoughts to push their way through like new shoots. Family above all, the moral education teacher had taught them, even though Xinying was a much better teacher.

Kai took out the wrinkled drawing from his pocket. It was no longer crispy. So many times he had crumpled it in anger and then smoothed it when he calmed down. Even tissue paper was stronger. His forefinger followed the lines Mei drew—the steady lines that formed the flower on her hair, the perfect circle of her head, the controlled details of the pendant on her neck. His finger came to a stop there. He knew now what he could do, had to do, for his family.

Chapter 27

Lee got in the passenger seat. He could have sat at the back, but that would be too superior for a mere off-duty chauffeur. The taxi moved away. This time, it was not his job to watch out for traffic or pedestrians. He sat back. The first light peeped over the rooftops. Market vendors stumbled along with their carts past townsfolk staggering out of their houses. All around, roosters greeted them with their persistent cries. Soon the stray dogs would comb the streets.

A little way after the fruit-seller's stall there was a narrow side street. The taxi turned into it and went down the lane. It was as if they had entered a forgotten world. After a couple of turnings, he arrived at the cul-de-sac where Da Laopan lived. Lee got out.

There was nobody about. Ah Sau must have gone to the market.

He headed straight toward the study. As expected, Da Laopan was already at his desk and looked up when Lee cast his weary shadow. The businessman had more gray hair than he remembered.

"You're back!" Laopan rose and waved him in. "Where's Han?"

Lee relayed the entire story of his journey. When he finished, Laopan was still for a long moment. Then he walked over to the pot Lee had left by the door.

"This is the antidote?"

"Yes. How's Ah Fu?"

"Getting worse." Da Laopan combed through the soil. "Your son did it for all five days?"

"Yes, Han only did one night."

"And Han ate one?

Lee nodded. "He looked like he went to sleep and never woke up."

Da Laopan picked up one of the closed shells. "Maybe boiling for one night was not enough. But five days, surely the poison's all gone by five days. But how can we tell?"

Some barking came over the wall. Usually Laopan paid no attention to the noise. This time his eyes lit up. "Let's try it out on the stray dogs."

In the far corner of the kitchen Ah Sau stowed the granite pestle and mortar. Lee bashed the shell and stuck a chopstick in the tiny hole. What he fished out reminded him of yellow bean paste; dull yellow and unappetizing. He found a couple of old plates and smeared them with as much of the paste as he could extract.

The back street was quiet. Across it by the rubbish heap sat a couple of flea-infested dogs. They were almost the same color as the contents on the plate. Lee put the plates down. The dogs wagged their tails. They stood up, looked down the road and back at him again. He waited for them to come over, but they kept looking down the street. A lone encumbered figure was coming toward them.

"Ah Sau!" Da Laopan called out.

"Laopan? What are you doing out here?" Ah Sau's body found new strength for the shopping.

"We're trying out the antidote on the strays," Lee said.

"Lee?" She cocked her head. "You're back! The antidote? Han's brought back the antidote? Where's Han?"

Lee glanced at Da Laopan, who moved toward Ah Sau and said in a voice he had only heard him use for his grandson. "Ah Sau, this is heavy, let me help you carry."

"No, no, no, I can manage. Is Han inside?"

"Let's go in first."

Ah Sau's grief was the screech of a thousand corn grinders, summoning Mrs. Laopan from her room. Even the legendary Great Yu from Sichuan could not control the flood from their eyes.

Lee and Da Laopan returned to the back street. Both plates were licked clean, the two dogs lying down. Lee crept toward them.

Chapter 28

The morning light, which had been steadily working its way up to greet the land, finally burst into his room, illuminating it with golden beams. Kai got up. Today was the day before the dumpling festival. The final day of the seed's infusion with earth.

The rope for tying Pig was hung on the post next to the gate. Kai had not used it on Pig for a long time, for he never strayed. But today was different. He picked up the rope and slung it into the basket with the rest of the items he had packed. He unlatched the gate. Together Kai and Pig journeyed toward the river.

At the bank, Kai began to shift the mound. Eventually he heard a rustle of dead leaves. Kneeling down, Kai brushed away the soil. At the bottom of the pit, the little parcels lay intact. The leaves that wrapped around the seeds had dried up.

"I knew I'd find you here," a familiar voice rang through the trees. Xinying appeared from downstream, where she had first discovered Kai with the 'football fruit.' Kai grinned. She looked at the parcel in his hand. "Is that it?" She jogged toward him.

Cradling the parcel, he grappled for the end of the leaf to unwrap without spilling the contents. In the end, he put the parcel on the ground and pulled off each leaf one by one.

"How does it look? Has it worked?" Xinying asked, between gasps.

He had not thought about what he was expecting to find after all this waiting. But if it were a legend like Xinying described, there should have been a flash of lightning and a loud rumble from the sky revealing a shiny skin and even a fragrant smell. But the flattened seeds looked just like the day they were buried—a dull chestnut color. Pig gave it a little sniff and wandered off. No smell either, not even a rotting one.

Kai looked at Xinying with a raised eyebrow. The s e nse o f anti-climax was also evident in her eyes. Then a twinkle, and the corners of her mouth curled. They b urst o ut l aughing t ogether a t the ludicrousness of their imagination.

Xinying wiped the giggles from her eyes. "What's next?"

"Let's put them in my basket," Kai said. "Oh, wait, let me empty it out first."

He turned his basket over and its contents fell out.

"Is that clean or dirty?" Xinying pointed to his neatly folded clothes and blanket on the ground.

"Who folds their dirty clothes?"

"Why have you brought them here then?"

Kai puffed out his chest. "I've decided," he said. "I'm going to find Ma."

"What?"

Chapter 29

"Remember my good luck pendant?" Kai pulled out the gold chain. "I've decided Ma needs it more."

"What?" Xinying's back was arched like a cat's. "Why?"

"She needs it to keep her job. Or if I'm too late, to find a new one."

"When did you decide that?"

"The day when I told you about the pendant, but I waited till today to leave so I can bring her these too." Kai scooped up the shells and turned toward his basket. "It was only a few more days, so I might as well. They've been treated exactly as the temple man instructed." He put the shells in the bottom of the basket.

"But they don't want them anymore."

"Ma needs the pendant, and I'm bringing it to her," he said. "Like you said, we all can choose what we do."

"But that's not what I meant!" Xinying's hands were on her hips.

Kai shook his head stubbornly. "She needs it to keep her job. Or this medicine will. Or both."

He waited for her comeback, but Xinying was quiet. An awkward silence hung between them.

"Okay, maybe I should test the medicine first," Kai said.

"No!" Xinying's reply was immediate. "It's not edible, remember? Uncle Liang told me—" She faltered. Xinying took a deep breath. "You promised him. Kai, we mustn't eat it. It was only for the school assembly, to finish what we started. But there is no proof it's safe to eat."

"We could see if the birds will eat it now."

"No. You promised."

"Okay, but I'm still bringing it to Ma. She can decide what to do. As long as she gets her lucky pendant."

Xinying was quiet for a moment. "You really want to give her the pendant?"

He nodded.

"So," Xinying picked up the rope. "What is this for?"

"I need that to harness Pig." Kai was glad the interrogation was over. "He's coming with me." He stretched out his hand.

Xinying passed the rope over. "Do you know the way?"

"Sort of. I know they take the overnight bus to the city. But I don't have any money, so I was going to ask Uncle. I know Ma and Pa send money to him for looking after me."

Pig sauntered toward them.

"Let's go and find him then," Xinying said. "I'll ask if I can come with you too."

"What?"

Chapter 30

Kai grabbed Pig with both arms and bore his eyes into Xinying's.

"You're my friend, I don't want you to go on that journey on your own." Xinying held Pig while he tied the rope.

Even if he had had his attention focused on Xinying, he would not have realized that behind her gesture of support she knew she had to think quickly to stop him. But stop him in a gentle manner.

"I don't abandon my friends like that." Xinying also knew the right words to convince him.

"Are you allowed?" Kai asked, trying not to sound too hopeful.

"I'll go and ask Uncle. He might let me, as Ahyi is back for a few weeks. She's really lucky. Apparently not all of them were allowed. It depended on which part of the sports shoes they were assembling." Xinying rambled on to veil her deception. "When do you want to set off?" She held up the basket for him. He put his arm round one of the cloth straps and wriggled his body to find the other strap.

"Now."

"All right," Xinying said weakly. "Walk back with me and we'll ask."

Uncle Liang was sitting in the front of his hut, shaving little pieces off a block of wood.

"Hello, Uncle Liang," they said to him in unison.

Uncle Liang looked up to see Kai beaming, but Xinying's face was furrowed.

Coming in front of Kai, she threw Uncle a strange look. Before he could work out what she was trying to say, she spoke, "Uncle, can I ask you something?" Without waiting for his reply, she walked toward the ladder of the hut, dropped her basket on the ground, and climbed into the hut.

Uncle Liang got up. "Wait here, Kai."

When they were safely out of earshot, Xinying explained Kai's pendant and their little experiment with the Dragon's Pearl Tree. "Uncle, he wants to go to the city and find his ma," Xinying said when she finished her account.

Uncle Liang narrowed his eyes.

"I didn't know how to talk him out of it, so I just told him I would come along. What should we do?"

Uncle Liang looked out of the doorway at the child below, who was running his fingers over the edges of the carved wood. He swiped a hand over his clipper-cut hair. After Yee Por's accident, it was even more important he continued to look out for Kai. He had promised Lee and Mei.

It had become a ritual, going to Kai's hut during the school day. He had been topping up Pig's water and food, but only enough to keep Kai from becoming suspicions. After dark, he would sneak up the mountain to make sure Kai was safely tucked up, however exhausted he was after a day in the fields. He often pondered on how he could gain Kai's trust. Yes, he could insist Kai stay with him. After all, it was what Lee and Mei wanted, but the child did not need any more top-down commands. He had been on the receiving end of a harsh decision, however logical or understandable it was. He felt abandoned and now he was guilt-stricken about Yee Por. From Xinying's account, day by day the boy had built a wall around himself. Inside the wall, he was crumbling bit by bit.

Now, this opportunity presented itself.

"How do we stop him without hurting his feelings? He still blames himself for Yee Por," Xinying said.

Uncle Liang turned round. In the shadows, his eyes gleamed. "Let me see what I can do. I might be able to change some things."

Chapter 31

Lee prodded a paw with a wooden stick. No reaction. He tried again, this time harder. No reaction. Da Laopan appeared from behind and kicked the dogs. They rolled and stayed limp. The old man buried his face in his hands. A muffled howl escaped.

The back door creaked. He dragged his hands away. Mrs. Laopan emerged.

"We've wasted our time," he said. "They are not for eating."

Mrs. Laopan went to her husband and they clung onto each other.

The light in Da Laopan's room was on through most of the night. Servants tiptoed and spoke in whispers. Despair hung over the household like the imminent war between thunderstorm and scorching sun. In the morning, staff were called to the front room. The couple appeared together, their faces translucent.

"We have decided to move to the country residence for a few weeks. I will make arrangements for the workers to speed up the renovations there." Da Laopan announced. "This city air is not good for the young master. Maybe the fresh country air in Qiang will be better. That's the least we can do for him."

Next to him, Mrs. Laopan was dabbing the inevitability from her eyes. The chill of wind swept through the room. This was the first time they had admitted the reality of their grandson's situation.

After the announcement, Mei accompanied Mrs. Laopan to the young master's room. Mrs. Laopan grieved by Ah Fu's side, leaving Mei to her own thoughts. She wondered how much longer she would be his ahma. Bad things seemed to follow her, ever since she left her pendant with Kai. At least, she assured herself, it was keeping Kai safe at home. Her heart missed a beat. Home was not too far from Qiang. She could visit when she was off, the last Sunday every month.

Chapter 32

Uncle Liang stepped out of the house again. "Kai, Xinying tells me you want to find your parents."

Kai's knees did a little dance in anticipation of the reunion. To Uncle Liang, he simply nodded.

"Do you know it's a long way away?" Uncle Liang sat down on his stool.

"We're not afraid of the long ride."

"It's not just the long ride—"

"I know my parents have sent you money in case I need it, so I thought…"

"Well, I wasn't thinking about the money," Uncle Liang said. "The bus journey…after you get off the overnight bus from here," Uncle Liang parted his hands to show the distance traveled, "you have to take an all-day bus." His arms parted even further. "And finally, another overnight bus." His hands were as far apart as his arms could stretch. "When it stops, you'll be in the big city."

It was Kai's turn to widen his eyes. He did not notice Pig was trying to sniff at Uncle Liang's outstretched fingers. Before he could respond, Xinying spoke what was on his mind.

"So many buses? I thought the bus from here simply went straight to the city," Xinying said. "How would we know where to get on and off?"

"Yes, it'll be complicated. Not a trip for children to take on their own, especially for their first time." Uncle Liang dropped his arms to his side. "Your parents sent me money for emergencies, not bus tickets to go and find them." He was silent for a moment, then he sucked in the air. "I'm sorry, Kai. I can't let you go."

Deep inside him, a part of Kai wept. It had been so long since anyone had disallowed him to do anything. Could it really be that someone other than Ma would care enough about him?

But this was buried within a heartbeat. What right did Uncle Liang have to stop him? He wasn't Ma or Pa. Before he could glare at him, Uncle Liang spoke again.

"But I have an idea. I know Da Laopan has a country house in Qiang. I'll take you there. We'll ask the caretaker there for help."

It never occurred to Kai that Uncle Liang could simply call the caretaker to make the enquiries. He did not know Uncle Liang had a different motive to make the trip down the mountain. "How can he help?"

"Maybe they have an idea if or when Da Laopan is coming this summer." Uncle Liang put away the sharp chisels. "I know it's still a little early—"

"Maybe they send people backward and forward from the city," Xinying said. "And we'll ask if they could deliver your parcel for us."

"Or if I can catch a lift with them to the city," Kai said. "I want to give it to Ma personally."

Uncle Liang did not meet his eyes, but raised his eyebrows in a manner Kai was sure meant that he had made a good suggestion.

Chapter 33

Uncle Liang slapped a hand on each knee and straightened his back. "As it's the public holiday tomorrow, I can take you to see my friend in Zang village. Do you remember Uncle Pak zooming in his new truck during Chinese New Year? He'll be able to drive us to Qiang." Uncle Liang stood up. "Let's pack some provisions for our excursion. It'll take us a whole day to get to Zang. We'll camp for the night by the Great Lake." He went back to his hut.

Kai hung back and rubbed Pig's belly. He felt he had grown two inches. Uncle Liang had not agreed with his initial plans, but instead of brushing him off as silly ideas as Pa would have, he had worked with him to find an alternative solution, like he was worth listening to.

They went the way to the river and walked further downstream until Kai saw a narrow wooden bridge. He let the harnessed Pig trot ahead of him. Walking one behind the other, they crossed over to the other side. Even Pig managed to cross it without slipping and falling over.

Kai had never been this way before. He made his way through the thick bushes. Every step brought his feet onto creepers that came up to his shins. Uncle Liang pretended they were snakes and stomped on them for him. After a couple of times, he copied Uncle Liang's big strides and heavy steps. Uncle, in turn, made squelchy noises each time he let his foot land heavily, as if squashing them. Like the unseen crickets rubbing their wings in a rhythmic fashion, their steps downhill went in synchrony. At one point, Uncle Liang told him to look up at the baby dragons. He glimpsed a pair of fluttering birds no bigger than his middle finger. Xinying was right. Uncle Liang was a lot of fun. He made the forest come alive.

Then Kai stopped. Ahead of them was the fattest tree he had ever seen. "What is that?" he cried.

Uncle Liang's voice softened to a hollow. "The Ancient Trap. It ensnared the Phoenix Maiden a thousand years ago. Let's go and set her free." He winked at Kai and stretched his hand toward Pig's rope. "Give Pig to me. You two can run ahead and take a look. Be careful not to fall. I don't want those precious shells rolling down the hill."

"Or the snakes will swallow them straightaway," Xinying said.

"Let's go, Xinying!" Kai charged downhill, he had not run like this for a long time. The last time he felt this exhilarated was a year ago, before the drought came.

They got close up to the tree. It did not have a fat trunk but was in fact made up of a cluster of trees. Xinying pointed out that it was more like a maze tree. No wonder Uncle called it an Ancient Trap. It grew out humbly enough, with its thin trunk. As it grew, it spread its branches and dropped vines downward. When the vines reached the ground, they anchored themselves, forming a secondary trunk. Over time, several of them settled randomly around the primary one. From afar, it looked like a tree with a fat trunk; but up close it was a maze of intertwined branches.

They weaved through the forest of maze trees until they reached the tall trees. Standing majestically at the gateways out of the forest, these opened like umbrellas at the top and towered over all the other trees. Past these gates the foliage was replaced by grass, barren like a desert after the excitement of the thick forest. Beyond the prairie, the Great Lake shimmered.

By the time they reached the Great Lake, the sun had nearly disappeared. They quenched their thirst and replenished their stocks of water. In the ebbing light, Kai and Xinying searched for dry wood. Uncle Liang set up a frame to hang the pot.

Insects in the foliage welcomed them with their evening song. A long, shrill note was followed by a shorter one, alternating this way and gaining tempo until the notes merged into a long tone. Then a pause and it started again. Before long, the flames danced to the rhythm of the acappella song. They ate their thick porridge in the flickering shadows. Soon the fire slowed to soothing embers. They yawned goodnight and drifted into their own misty lands.

Kai dreamt he was in Uncle Liang's house, having breakfast with him and Auntie Liang, Xinying, and the twins. They were in their school uniforms. They were only eating plain rice and pickled vegetables, but it was a feast. Pig was living below the hut, except Pig was a dragon that could not fly. Then they were eating the same food again, except this time it was dinner. After dinner, they did their homework together. When it was dark, they all slept on the wooden floor, head to toe, until Uncle woke them and said it was time to get up.

Kai opened his eyes and saw Uncle Liang's broad face. He floated a smile back. It had been so long since he woke up to someone else at home.

"Did you sleep well?" Uncle asked in a manner like it was a question he asked Kai every morning, as though Kai was part of his family living in his home. "Time to wake up now. Dawn's the best time to set off." His breath almost formed a mist in front of him.

Up in the trees, birds celebrated the end of the night. The water adjacent reminded Kai where he was, not the new life with Uncle Liang. His body felt heavy. Kai forced his leaden body up. They set off.

Uncle Liang did not notice Kai's heavy footsteps, for his own were light. Kai's smile earlier told him his aim for this journey was working.

A pair of eyes at the front of the willow-colored boat watched them approach the bank. A couple of passengers were getting on. The old ferryman looked at Kai and Xinying kindly before he turned to Uncle Liang for payment.

The young assistant stood by the thick rope tied to the boat, his arms folded and legs slightly apart. He looked a few years older than Kai. Anyone who had a notion of avoiding payment would be put off by the stern look. If that were not enough, the bulges on his upper arms should convince them. Kai could feel his sullen eyes moving up and down, scrutinizing and searching. He fidgeted uncomfortably. The good-luck pendant peeping through the gap of his shirt caught the morning sun. He thought he saw the assistant's eyes flicker, but when he looked again his steady gaze unnerved him. Kai glanced away.

A moment later, the ferryman nodded his head.

Uncle Liang picked Pig up. "Who's first?"

The assistant pulled the rope against the stump, holding it steady for them to walk up the plank.

Kai ran up it. He left Xinying to tiptoe behind, and Uncle Liang came up last with Pig. He did not see the old ferryman get on board to start the engine, so he threw his hands to his ears and screamed when he heard a sudden growl.

"What was that?" He looked round for the source of the sound, but the thunderous noise was now replaced by a rolling groan, drowning his voice. Nobody else seemed worried. The young assistant released the rope from the jetty and they moved away from the edge.

"Can I go to the front?" He fixed his eyes ahead on the open waters as if he might miss something.

"Of course, but I'll be here at the back." Uncle Liang patted the wooden seat next to him.

Kai looked at Uncle Liang quizzically.

Chapter 34

It took a week for Da Laopan to finalize the new renovation schedule at the country cottage, and it took the builders another month to finish the work. Finally, they moved. By now, Ah Fu had difficulty breathing, gulping the heavy factory air.

Lee drove the family to Qiang. Without Han, extra responsibility fell on him. He unloaded their luggage. There were several essentials they needed for the cottage, so while Mei unpacked, he made his way to the shops in the center. At the junction, people blocked his way at every turn. This was not the place to be polite. As soon as he spotted the tiniest gap, he had to shove his shoulders forward immediately, otherwise someone else would step in to occupy it. He pushed his way through the throng, voices surrounding him.

"There were two groups of them."

"Two men arrived on a bike."

"...a deep scar down his eye."

"Ma, what's going on? I can't see."

"Ai, children! Don't ask so many questions!"

Suddenly everyone surged forward, and Lee found himself being brought along in that direction. It reminded him of the days when he worked in the sugar cane factory, being squeezed like a cane through the rollers. The crowd in front had stopped, but the masses behind continued to push forward. Then the rollers stopped.

Through the slit between the heads and shoulders in front of him, Lee still could not see what the holdup was. He stood on his toes. Then he saw it.

A man lying on the street was being lifted onto an ambulance trolley. His head was shaved. A deep scar ran from his forehead down to his cheek. His front was covered with red stains. A pendant dangled from his neck. Lee blinked hard. It couldn't be. He had to take a closer look.

The medics were pushing the trolley toward the ambulance, which was parked along the intersection, closer to him than them. He might make it there before them if the people let him through easily.

"I'm sorry." Lee shoved past a man, keeping an eye on the trolley.

"Excuse me," he said to another, who frowned at him and turned away without budging.

By now the medics had reached the vehicle and the door

opened. Other people at the back were edging forward, stretching their necks to catch a glimpse of the action, closing any spaces for him to squeeze across.

"Let me through. I need to get closer!" Lee jostled through.

Faces turned toward him. The people in front of him stepped back, some murmured. But it was too late. The door slammed and the ambulance whizzed away with its siren.

Lee stared after the ambulance. He must have imagined it, but it was so like Mei's pendant. That must have been a coincidence. How could Kai's pendant end up here in Qiang? The crowd dispersed, and Lee hurried with his errands. He returned to the cottage and called Uncle Liang. But it was Mrs. Liang who answered the call and informed him Ah Liang had taken the two older children to Zang for the weekend. Zang village was between their hamlet and Qiang.

"If Kai's in Zang, then it couldn't have been your pendant," Lee said to Mei.

"But what if something has happened to them, to Kai, and the robber took the pendant and came to Qiang?" Mei said. "You know what the story says; if the wrong hands take the pendant, ill fortune will befall them. You said that man was injured. That's ill fortune."

"Come on, Mei. Surely not," Lee said.

Mei stayed silent.

"Surely that was just your grandmother's tall tale."

Mei sighed. "If only I could just see it. I wish there was someone who could help us. Who do we know in Qiang? Anyone?"

Her question jolted Lee's memory. "We do. Let's go to the police station and speak to Bai," Lee said. "Bai might be able to help us."

"Of course! Bai works at the police station, and I even showed him the pendant's scratch at Chinese New Year."

Bai was not available. The police officer at the reception said he was in the middle of a meeting. They waited. The waiting room consisted of four gray walls and two wooden benches, not that curtains and flowers would have made any difference. Finally he came out looking tired. When they explained what had happened, he took them into a quiet room.

"That's what I've been working on all afternoon. There was an incident earlier, a gang fight. We made quite a few arrests," Bai looked at Lee. "The youth you saw, Lohng, he died on the way to hospital."

Mei gasped.

"It was the same boy I told you about at Chinese New Year, the one with the long scar down his face. Turns out he'd just traveled from the Great Lake this morning."

"So he would have been in Zang before he came here!" Mei cried. "Something's happened to Kai!"

"Can we see the pendant?" Lee asked.

Bai nodded. "According to one of the other youths, Lohng had just robbed someone of a pendant today. So if you can describe it accurately, we'll say we've identified the rightful owners and return it to you."

Bai took them to another officer, and Mei described the pendant to him, the gold chain, the circular jade, the character in the middle, and even the scratch at the back. The officer nodded his head. Mei signed the papers with shaking hands and took the pendant from the duty officer.

"What did the youth say about the robbery?" Lee asked.

"Only that they ambushed a boy for his gold chain."

Mei's hand flew over her mouth. "What about Liang or Xinying?"

"It sounded like he was on his own." Bai's voice was grim.

Mei stifled a sob. Lee put his arm around her.

"I'm really sorry, Mei. But I'll make some enquiries," Bai promised. "I've got to track down Lohng's younger brother. Jian doesn't go to school around here, I've been told. Ai, he's only ten years old. Parents left, grandparents gone, and now—"

Lee linked arms with Mei, and they made their way back.

"It's another omen," Mei said.

Lee remained silent. He knew it had been a grueling afternoon for her.

"Things have really not been going well lately," Mei said. "So much has happened in such a short space of time—Yee Por, Han, Ah Fu's worse, and now this. How did it end up like this?"

They turned off from the main road onto the unsealed path leading to the country home. In contrast to the mêlée earlier, silence deafened the front courtyard, as if they were already in mourning.

"I'm going to lose this job when he goes, won't I? What am I going to do then?"

"Shh, don't talk like that."

"I thought I was making our lives better by coming here." Her usual soft voice broke into a sob. "I'm being punished. I made the wrong choice. I should never have left Kai. I've let him down, and now he's gone."

Chapter 35

"I'm not very good on boats." Uncle Liang explained.

Kai looked at Xinying, who raised her eyebrows and shrugged. He turned back to Uncle Liang.

"I'm fine on the steady ground, but on water my stomach doesn't feel too good," Uncle Liang said. "It's less choppy at the back."

Kai did not really understand what Uncle Liang meant, except that he was staying put at the back. He turned to Xinying. "Are you coming?"

She looked unsure but nodded her head.

"Come on, Pig. I want to be in the front."

Kai weaved his way across the boat. He cast a curious glance at the other two passengers. The first one had an upturned nose and a mouth curled downward in a cruel smirk. The other had a shaved head that accentuated his square jaw. His slanted eyes met Kai's briefly before looking away. Had Kai been more world-wise, he would have spotted their intimidating tattoos sooner and avoided any eye contact. Instead, his gaze loitered long enough for him to notice the vicious scar cutting the eyebrow through to his lower cheekbone. This frightened Kai, and he returned his concentration to keeping his balance, unaware that Scar-cheek was now watching him.

Making his way to the front, Kai knelt on the seat so that he could take in the view. The wind blew in his face with the occasional splash from the waters. He closed his eyes to absorb the refreshing sensation. Next to him sat a quivering Pig, whose ears were pulled back like he wanted to pull the brakes on the ferry. They stayed like this for a while.

The wind picked up slightly and made waves on the water. Sometimes the boat rose up at the wrong time and hit the oncoming wave full-on. That stopped it for a split second, and then the boat continued again. Kai laughed out loud when he was thrown forward and backward by the waves.

Xinying, who had been very quiet throughout, finally spoke. "I think I know what Uncle means. I don't feel too good," she said in a faint voice. "I'm going back to sit with him."

There was a distinct paler shade on Xinying's face. She got up and staggered to the back.

When they were halfway across the lake, the young assistant

came and sat with Kai. He acknowledged Kai with a slight nod and pulled his lips somewhat outward at the edge. He did not say anything, but started to stroke Pig. After a while, he leaned toward Kai and spoke in a low tone. "I've just counted the money. Your uncle did not pay for you."

Kai gawked at him. "But he let all of us on."

"Because you're so tiny. The old man is too kind and people take advantage of him," the youth said. "But we are not a charity." He let his eyes drop down under Kai's chin. "If you give me the pendant, we will talk no more of this."

Kai had to convince himself he heard it right the first time.

Before he could reply, the young man continued in his low whisper. "I know you're wearing it under your shirt. You can't hide it from me. I don't want any trouble, just payment for what's due."

Panic rose up Kai's esophagus.

"I just want my dues," the ferry youth said. "You use our ferry, you pay your fare. I don't really want your cursed pendant, but I haven't got a choice. That's all you've got. "

Kai shifted his feet to get off the bench. "Let me ask Uncle Liang."

"No, don't do that!" The youth grabbed his shoulders and pulled him close. From behind, they looked like best friends enjoying the ride together. "Your uncle's sitting too close to the old man," he said. "He'll overhear, and it'll upset him."

Kai recoiled. His upper arm hurt. It was the big boys at school all over again.

"He thinks it's more important to keep his customers happy and charge nothing for kids. But we still have to carry you across. You're not good business for me."

Much as he was a bully, the young man was right. It was not fair his passage was not paid, but he had set out on this journey to give Ma the pendant. He had nothing else he could pay for the ride. Apart from the pendant, all he had was the antidote and Pig, and he could not give up either of them.

Kai prayed Uncle Liang and Xinying would see he was being cornered. But without eyes behind his back, he did not know Xinying was leaning against Uncle Liang with her eyes closed. Neither could he see that in the shadows under his flat cap, Uncle Liang also had his eyes shut. Nor was he aware that Scar-cheek was watching the pair of them.

"Tell you what." The ferry youth's voice became as buttery as yak fat. "There is a pawnshop in the next town. I will leave it there with them. When your parents return me your fare, I'll get your pendant back, deal?"

Kai had never heard of a pawnshop. But he understood his mother's pendant would be kept in a holding place until he could pay for his passage. That sounded fair. But how could he continue this journey if he did not have his pendant?

His head groaned like the ferry engine. The old ferryman had to be out of earshot before he could ask Uncle Liang for money. Then he would exchange his pendant back right away, without the need to go to the holding place. That should work. He just had to make sure the youth did not head off without them.

With one hand holding on to Pig, he used the other to undo the pendant. Naturally undoing a clasp with only one hand was awkward. The young assistant watched his clumsy attempts for what seemed like an eternity.

"Here, let me hold your pig for you so both your hands are free." He wrapped his arm around Pig and edged closer to Kai, closing any gaps between them so the transaction was carried out discreetly.

Kai unfastened the chain. He lifted it away from his neck. In that brief moment, the gold sparkled and was spotted by a pair of eyes watching from behind.

The youth put the pendant in his pocket. "Remember, this is our secret. You mustn't let the old man know."

They eventually reached the other side. The other two passengers jumped off even before the boat was tied to the wooden stump. They disappeared round the bend. The youth tied the boat to the jetty, winked at Kai, and jogged off in the same direction.

"Hey!" Kai shouted.

"Don't worry. I can help you," the old ferryman said.

He took Kai's hand, and Kai jumped off the ferry. By this time the youth was nowhere in sight. Uncle Liang and Xinying were so relieved

Chapter 36

D espite their brisk walk, they did not see him.

"The trail to the village is flat. We should have been able to spot him easily," Uncle Liang said.

"Could he have taken a shortcut?" Xinying asked.

Uncle studied the path they had just trekked. "Maybe, if he had climbed up that hill we just walked round. See that pair in the distance, the other two passengers on the ferry? That'll explain why those two are so far ahead of us. They must have taken the shortcut.

"He must have been even quicker than those two. I saw him run off as soon as he landed. We'd better hurry and catch him," Kai said.

But Uncle Liang pulled Kai and Xinying toward him and spoke in a low voice. "See that tree just ahead, surrounded by bushes? Let's go there and sit there for a minute. I think he might be hiding until he thinks it is safe, and then he'll go back to the boat.

"You mean he wasn't going to the pawnshop?"

"That's what I'm afraid of. Let's hope I'm wrong."

They sat quietly for a long while, watching the hill.

"I think he must have reached the pawnshop by now," Kai finally said.

Uncle Liang's shoulders dropped. "Yes, I suppose we'd better catch up with him." Uncle got up and his body rustled against the bushes such that nobody heard him when he mumbled, "Where can he be hiding?"

As they arrived at the entrance of the village, a three-wheeled motor vehicle going in the opposite direction roared past them, throwing up dirt from the tracks. If they had not been blinded by the dust from the bike, they would have spotted that the riders were the same people on the boat. When the dust settled, they opened their eyes and continued their way into the village.

Zang village was very much like Pumi village, but as he had never been there, he did not know that. Kai simply thought he had stepped into another world. Each with their baskets on their backs, they squeezed through the throng of people. Kai had no idea where they were heading. His face pressed against Uncle Liang's basket, secretly relieved that Uncle Liang was in front with Pig and Xinying was close behind. Sandwiched between them, he felt safe in this bewildering place. Even Pig was quiet. For once, he was glad his basket was deep; with the medicine tucked under his blanket at the bottom, no amount of shoving could knock them out.

The place was full of buildings in stone and brick, standing side by side in a terrace manner. The overhanging upper floors provided shelter for the shops below, forming a common corridor for shopkeepers to display their wares. People jostled by. Kai simply moved with the flow, listening to Xinying and Uncle Liang talking over his head.

"There're so many people," Xinying said. Someone pushed her from behind. Xinying almost squashed Kai's basket. She positioned her hands on Kai's shoulders as if they were playing trains.

"It's market day here. We can't locate him in this crowd," Uncle Liang said. "We will have to go to the pawnshop and see if he's taken it there."

A lady walked past them. On her back, like almost everyone else here, was a deep basket. A little child was in it. This scene jolted Kai's memory. He remembered being in one of those baskets once when he was little. He must have been about three years old then. There were lots of people, and the cacophony was so frightening he started screaming. Now, he might be older, but in this swarm of people he felt like screaming again. Uncle Liang was right. There was no way they were going to find the man with his pendant here.

"Where is the pawnshop?" Xinying asked.

"There's someone I know we can ask. That's where we're heading."

The air cooled. People around them dispersed. They were in a huge open square. In the middle, stalls lined in rows. Everything was on sale here: home needs like brooms, stools, and baskets; farming needs like seeds and hoes; pretty things like flowers, embroidery, thread, and handwoven cloths. Uncle Liang stopped in front of the stall with wooden figurines. In front of them on the right was a carving of an old man fishing. Next to it was a dragon chasing a fire ball. Kai longed to run his fingers along its scales and clawed feet.

"Ni hao!" Uncle Liang released his basket with one arm while holding Pig with the other. Kai took Pig from him.

"Liang Xiong! I wasn't expecting you here." The man running the shop had a pouch round his waist. "I thought I wouldn't see you till Pumi market day."

"It's the Dumpling Festival, so we had a little excursion." Uncle Liang put one hand each on Xinying and Kai's shoulder.

The man smiled at them and turned back to Uncle Liang. "I've got good news for you. I sold your other masterpiece." He pointed under the stall. "The new owner will collect it later on, but he's paid me already."

Kai peered under the table. What he saw nearly made him drop Pig. Sitting in a cardboard box were the three men of good life; one surrounded by animals, an old one carrying a peach, and the third wore a hat with two side flaps.

"Excellent!" Uncle Liang rubbed his unsymmetrical hands

together. "Did you get a good price for it?"

"I always do when it's your carving." The man reached in his front pouch and took out some notes. "Here we are, your payment." He handed the money over to Uncle Liang, who counted it and then beamed at the man.

"Have you got something else for me to sell?"

"I do." Uncle Liang reached in the basket and retrieved a large parcel wrapped in cloth. Gingerly he put it on the table, peeled away the cloth, and lifted it high.

Xinying leaned toward Kai. In his arms, Pig was wriggling and stretching as if he was trying to get close to her. "You'll love this one," Kai heard Xinying whisper into his ear.

It was a bamboo windchime underneath a wooden Chinese junk.

"Look at the ropes on the sails, the planking and the ripples of waves," the man said. "It must have taken you hours!"

"Ai, many hours of despair, carving and re-carving," Uncle Liang said.

Just then, the breeze picked up. The bamboos of different lengths hit the middle piece as they danced. They sang, lifting the soul.

"Wonderful! Exquisite!" The man clapped his hands. "This will definitely sell. Tourists will love this one." He took it from Uncle Liang and hung it at the front corner of the stall. "Now everyone can admire this." The enchanting pieces swayed in the breeze, throwing out dulcet tunes.

"So, on this lovely sunny day, where are you off to now?"

"We're looking for the pawnshop," Uncle Liang said. "But I'm not sure where it is."

"Just head toward the south side." He pointed to his right. "Second street from where the hired trucks are."

"Oh, that's handy, we're heading that way next," Uncle Liang said.

They bade goodbye to the man.

Uncle Liang led them across the square. "Kai, you can let Pig walk for a bit now. It's not going to be so crowded where we're going."

Here, the vendors were spread out a bit more, selling things that needed space, like a lady with numerous basins on the ground, each with a fish or two in it. The basins were not big enough for the fish to swim, just enough to keep them alive. Or the man selling huge baskets to collect the harvests. Or live geese and chickens.

They went down a quieter lane. Like all the other shops, the doors had carved wooden panels. A few feet in front of the shop, two pillars on either end supported the room that hung over the corridor above. The wooden window panels on the ground level were equally pretty, with simple but effective straight bars crisscrossing each other. One in particular had metal frames. To Kai, it looked like a prison.

Uncle Liang stepped inside. The shop counters were so high only he could see what was over them. "Did anyone bring in a jade pendant today? Maybe in the last hour or so?" Uncle Liang asked. In a lower voice, more to himself, he said, "It'll be a miracle if he did."

Chapter 37

"Jade?" The woman behind the counter looked up through her glasses. "No." She went back to reading her newspaper.

Uncle Liang beckoned Kai over and lifted him as if he were a bouncy toddler. "Is your Ma's pendant here?"

It was a glass counter of gold jewelry and watches so dazzling they hurt his eyes.

"Why do they have to make it so high?" Xinying asked. "I can't see anything."

In the corner were some green stones; earrings, bracelets, cylindrical and rectangular pendants, and even ones carved into characters. But no circular pendant with Ma's maiden surname etched in the middle. Kai went back over all the items, row by row, column by column. "It's not here," he said at last.

"Didn't I tell you that already? Is there something wrong with your ears?" the woman spoke again.

"Sorry to have troubled you." Uncle Liang lowered Kai to the ground, ran his fingers over his black hair, and rubbed the back of his neck. He put his hand on Kai's shoulder and steered him out.

"She was so rude," Xinying said when they stepped outside. "She didn't even try to help us. Who would want to do business with her?"

But Kai did not hear her.

"He's obviously not here yet," Uncle Liang said, his voice heartening as chicken soup. "Must have got sidetracked with all these stalls. I'll wait here for him." Uncle read the sign on the door. "The pawnshop closes in an hour. The lad will have to be here by then. Why don't you two wander back to the market? Leave your baskets and Pig with me."

Kai did not see Xinying throw a worried look at Uncle Liang. Only she would have recognized that reassuring tone Uncle Liang liked to use when hiding something bad. "Come on, Kai. Let's go and check this place out."

They walked past a stall with silvery bracelets and stone necklaces. Xinying gushed. It was hard not to think about the pendant, but Kai remembered her inspirational words about not letting obstacles get in the way. At the next stall, some men were weaving baskets, so he said, "I wonder if they can make one to put on Pig's back?"

"Where did you get that idea from?"

"Uncle," Kai said. "Pig has so much energy, he thought he could help me carry the water back."

Xinying chuckled. In the air, he smelled deep-fried dumplings and steamed noodles. He almost tasted the crunchy snow pears and sweet persimmon when they passed the stall displaying red and yellow fruit in pyramids.

In a tiny gap between the fruit stall and medicinal stall, some carrots and green leafy vegetables were laid neatly in a couple of flat, open baskets. A girl about Xinying's age squatted down by her produce. The faraway, vacant look on her face contrasted the vibrant atmosphere and joyful chattering. She turned and looked in his direction. In her eyes, he thought he recognized that lonely anguish he knew too well. Kai blinked. When he opened his eyes, the girl only returned his gaze with a stony face. He did not want to linger or explore anymore.

They went back and waited with Uncle Liang. After some time, the surly shopkeeper shuttered the windows and locked up. Kai sank on the pavement. How could both man and pendant have vanished? The pendant was supposed to curse thieves and find its way back to him.

Chapter 38

When the ferry assistant woke up, he was sore at the base of his neck. Cool air rushed up his smooth face, warning him to open his eyes. Above him, he heard the new leaves rub against one another. He was on the top of a hill. Below him, there was an empty plain heading toward Zang.

All at once he remembered where he was. He had managed to make an excuse with the old man and left as soon as they landed. He had looked back and seen he was out of sight of the traveling menagerie. They were still getting off the boat. Stepping off the path, he had made his way among the trees and bushes, where he was sure they would not follow. The damp soil had turned rockier as the ground rose. When he had reached the top, a noise made him turn round. He had caught a glimpse of two men. Then he had felt an exploding pain. Just before he passed out, one of the men had leaned toward him with a long scar down his face.

The pawnshop. That was where he had pretended to be heading. He put his hand in his pocket. It was empty. He jumped up. The ache at the back of his head blasted all over his skull. He grabbed his crown with both hands and squatted down again. When the pain subsided, he opened his eyes, but it was too excruciating to move his head. With his head hanging down, he could only see stones, dead leaves, and twigs. The lad cursed his robbers. He should have known to be wary of anyone with a long scar down their face, ferry passengers or not.

Chapter 39

"I'm sorry you lost it," Uncle Liang said.

His words were meant to comfort Kai, but they triggered the release. Bottled-up feelings all these months detonated. Like he was possessed, Kai ran to the pawnshop, grabbed its bars, and shook the gate. "Aaaaaahhhhhhhhh!"

Uncle Liang ran after him. "Kai!"

"Aaaaaahhhhhhhhh!" Kai did not stop. He did not care that the place had become a tableau and everyone was staring at him.

Uncle Liang's strong arms rounded him.

"It's all right, Kai," he said. "I'm sure Ma will understand."

"I want Ma!" Kai screamed, flailing his arms to break from Uncle Liang. "I want to find Ma! I want Ma!"

Uncle had sprouted extra arms. He elbowed and wriggled, but

Uncle's arms still encircled him. The furious battle faded, and Kai was reduced to sobs. "I want Ma. I want Ma. I miss her."

Uncle Liang stroked his head gently. "Shhh." He spoke softly into Kai's ears. "I know it's hard. I know it's hard. It's very hard. Shhh, it's alright. Uncle's here."

"Why did they have to go, Uncle? I miss them, really miss them. Miss them to death!" He clung on to Uncle Liang, his head buried in Uncle's broad chest.

"Life's been unfair to you."

He wasn't fighting anymore, but Uncle continued to hold him. Presently, a little pink snout came and sniffed. He whined. His master was upset. Kai reached out and stroked his floppy ear. The long tail wagged. Kai sat up and wiped his face. The grief lingered but he had offloaded the worst of it.

"Maybe, like you said, the pendant will find its way back to its owner again," Xinying said, but Kai knew now that he had been tricked.

"Shall we head back home?" Uncle Liang asked

Home. That inclusive word, where you know you can count on one another.

"We are relying on you, son," were Mei's last words before she left.

His eyes drifted over to his basket.

Chapter 40

"**W**e've come all this way," Kai said. "Can we bring the medicine to the cottage anyway? They might need it."

"If you like. Uncle Pak's place is just round the corner."

They emerged from that narrow lane. The sight that greeted Kai should have amazed him. By the side of the dirt track, a row of enormous vehicles were parked. One was a three-wheeled bicycle with a low box at the back to transport large items. The one next to it was painted orange and also had three wheels. It had the front of a motor bike, but the back of a pickup truck. The last one was the largest, a red pickup bed towed by a reliable looking four-wheeled farm tractor. Squatting by the roadside were a couple of men in white singlets and black trousers. Another was next to the red vehicle, securing long bamboos with rope. Kai remembered him from Chinese New Year. He was the man who caused much excitement when he drove the new lorry to Yee Por's house.

"Stay here for a minute." Uncle Liang walked across the street and called. "Pak!"

The man by the red vehicle looked up and laughed out loud. "Ah-Liang, why are you here today?"

"Came to find you," Uncle Liang made his way toward Pak. "I need a favor. See that boy over there?" Uncle Liang tilted his head in Kai's direction. "Lee and Mei's son. He's been living on his own since Yee Por died. Now he wants to go and find his parents in the city."

"Oh, dear," said Pak. "Not another one."

"Thankfully, I've managed to stop him so far, but it's not over yet."

"What do you mean?"

"He wanted to give his parents something, so I suggested we go to the country house of their boss. I'm sure no one's there, but I needed an excuse to spend some time with him and convince him to come and live with us. The cottage is in Qiang. Going there gives me a couple of days to win him round."

"Do you mean Da Laopan, the great factory owner?"

Uncle Liang nodded.

"I heard they're coming here earlier this year," Uncle Pak said. "In fact, they might even have arrived, as the renovators have gone." Uncle Pak leaned toward Uncle Liang and dropped his voice. "I heard he's brought his grandson there to die."

"Let's not say that to the boy. Can you give us a lift there? "

Kai saw the pair had finished talking and were coming toward them.

"Come along now, hop on the back." When Uncle Pak smiled, his mouth filled his entire face. "Uncle Liang and I will sit in front, there should be plenty of space for you in the back."

The bamboos were secured lengthwise, jutting out the back and leaving a slanted den for Pig to hide under. A couple of low stools opposite beckoned Kai and Xinying. Kai dropped his basket next to Uncle Liang's at the top end.

"This'll be fast, so fast you'll feel the wind on your face," Uncle Liang said.

"The roads can be quite bumpy, so hold on tight," Uncle Pak said. Kai gripped the contents in his pocket so hard Mei's drawing crushed round the marble. The engine roared the dirt off the ground. They zoomed off, traveling in the same direction as Scar-cheek's bike earlier on, but not knowing it, of course.

Chapter 41

The pickup seemed to go over humps and bumps forever. Trees whizzed past. They passed many travelers walking to or back from Zang village. Even further away, someone herded yaks by the side of the road.

Then there they were, the stately gates into Qiang.

If he had felt tired from the journey, the sight ahead rejuvenated him. Compared to Zang village, this place seemed to have a polish to it. Vivid red lanterns hung from above. The designs on the wooden doors and windows were more elaborate. Here they even decorated the supporting pillars in front of the shops. The truck stopped to let a peddler cross the road with his cart. On the left, sweet fragrance drifted from a shop with flowers, their pillars painted in bright red, orange, and yellow.

"Look at that shop over there."

Kai followed the direction of Xinying's finger to the shop on their right. Round its pillars, bright colors of soft fabric draped. Plain cotton and silk blended with the intricate embroidery of lace. The peddler had crossed the road, and the truck moved. The fabric shop was behind them, but Xinying adjusted her position and kept her focus on it.

"My ma said she'd take me there to make a qipao one day." There was a glow in her eyes. "When I'm sixteen."

They moved through the streets, made a couple of turns, and arrived at a boulevard. Shop-houses lined both sides, all the way to the main junction. You would never have known there had been a street fight earlier on. Peddlers pushed their carts, calling out their wares and fine foods. Servants hurried along. They came to the crossroad and turned into a quiet unsealed street. At the end of the lane, two sparking pillars stood. A pile of renovation debris was dumped in front of them. Behind the pillars, was a freshly painted manor, its low roof endowed with shiny gray tiles.

Uncle Pak pulled up by the proud pillars. He turned off the engine, but the rumble continued in Kai's ears. The two uncles got out. They went behind to drop the back panel. Kai got up, but his legs could not move. He leaned against the side panel with tingling feeling on his buttocks, as if he were still juddering on the gravel roads. His face felt like it had been laid out to dry.

"Kai?" a female voice asked.

The uncles turned round and saw two familiar figures running toward them. Kai fell into Mei's arms.

"Mama!"

"Is it really you?" Mei embraced Kai so hard she was crushing him. "Thank heavens you're safe! We were so worried."

"I missed you! Missed you to death!"

"Uncle Bai said you were robbed. We thought the worst when we saw the pendant."

"The pendant?" Kai pulled away.

"What happened? How did you get separated?"

"What did you say about the pendant?"

"It's right here, look." Mei's fingers fumbled round her neck and the jade appeared from her top. "I got it back from the police. It was Uncle Bai, remember him at New Year? He was the officer in charge."

"The ferry boy was arrested?" Uncle Liang asked.

Lee shrugged. "Bai didn't say he was a ferry boy. He said he was one of the regular delinquents. He's got a long scar down his face."

"That's not the ferry boy, but he was on the ferry with us," Kai said. "Sitting near the front with me."

"But it was the ferry boy who took the pendant from you," Uncle Liang said.

"So the ferry boy robbed Kai, and this youth was also on the boat. He saw what happened and robbed the ferry boy?" Lee said.

"What happened to the ferry boy?" Kai asked

"What happened to the youth?" Xinying asked at the same time.

"I don't know about the ferry boy, but the youth was in Qiang earlier, in a fight," Lee said. "That was how we found the pendant. They were carrying him into the ambulance. I saw it round his neck."

"He's in the hospital? Will they arrest him when he gets out?"

"He died on the way to hospital."

Kai gaped at the heirloom. He glanced at Xinying and shifted his eyes back to the pendant.

"Wow, it's really true. The pendant…" Xinying said.

"That harm will go to those who steal it, and it will find its way back to us somehow," Mei said.

"So glad you're all safe and well." Lee ruffled Kai's hair.

"So glad we didn't lose the pendant," Kai said.

"Kai was determined to come and find you." Xinying dangled her legs at the edge of the pickup bed. "He wanted to give you the pendant and the antidote."

"Yes, yes! The seeds are ready now, for the young master." Kai broke free and headed back to the pickup.

"Seeds? You mean the seeds of the Great Fire Tree?"

"You didn't—"

"I made sure he didn't." Xinying passed his basket down.

Kai turned toward his parents. "I didn't eat any. Uncle said we can't, but I treated them properly. Maybe…"

His parents' eyes withered, for at this moment Da Laopan came out.

"Who are these people?"

"Laopan, this is our son."

Kai drifted to his parents' side.

"The one who helped…"Da Laopan could not finish his sentence.

"I finished the treatment Uncle Han started," Kai said.

Beside him, Mei drew her breath. He pulled his shoulders back with pride. It never occurred to him she still saw him as the boy who hid behind her when strangers spoke to him. With the return of the pendant, nothing daunted him.

"What do you mean 'finished the treatment?'"

"I did everything properly."

"Properly?" Da Laopan raised his eyebrows at Lee and Mei. "When your father brought back the nuts they were—"

"Not finished."

"Tell me what you did, exactly. Don't leave out anything."

"I boiled them, then left them to soak in the hot water, cooling down slowly overnight, like Uncle Han did. But because he left after the first night, I…er…Xinying," Kai glanced over to Xinying, who smiled and nodded,"helped me. We both changed the water and did it again, boiling and soaking." Kai circled his right hand like a spiral. "We did it five times. Pa brought some back then, but they still had to be buried with ashes, by the tree, for forty days—"

"Forty days?" Da Laopan, Lee, and Mei said all at the same time.

Kai nodded. "That's what the paper said, forty days. "He rummaged in his basket.

"No, no, I believe you. I know what the instructions were." Laopan's eyelids flapped like a paper fan. "I just didn't think that step was necessary."

But Kai did not hear him. He pulled out a wrinkled paper, unfolded it, and pointed at the bottom for Laopan. "So we wrapped them in big leaves and buried them next to the tree. Even Pig helped."

Kai held out his basket for them to see the end product. Da Laopan took a nut and contemplated it. Like everyone else, Kai held his breath.

After what felt like an eternity, Laopan finally spoke. "Boy, I assume you haven't tested it."

"No."

"Glad to hear that." Laopan turned to Lee. "You didn't tell him?"

"He told me," Uncle Liang said. "Except it wasn't a good time to tell Kai." Uncle paused. "We had an incident at the village, it was a difficult time. But the fruit was buried in the ground by then, and he'd promised me he wouldn't do anything else with it. Xinying knew, and she kept a close eye on him."

Kai puckered his brow. "What's going on?"

"I'm afraid this fruit is poisonous," Da Laopan glanced at the parents. "Do you want to tell him, or should I?"

"Han never came back," Mei said. "We believe he ate some."

"What do you mean he never came back? How do you know he ate it if he didn't return?"

"Because I saw his dead body on my way back."

Color drained from Kai's face. Even the sun was clouded over. "That doesn't mean he ate it," he said, after a while.

"There was an opened shell next to his hand."

"He only did it for one night. It wasn't ready. The instructions said five nights."

"But the ones I brought back, that you boiled for five nights, we tested them on stray dogs. They too died after eating."

"So I'm afraid you've wasted your time," Da Laopan said.

"But you did not bury it on the tree's ground for forty nights. You brought it back in some soil. That's not the same."

"Enough lives have been lost. I won't be letting anyone else try them. We're throwing them away," Da Laopan said.

After all that, they would just give up and throw the seeds away? Kai pressed his lips until the pink color faded. Mei moved toward him, the chain on her front glinted in the sun. The pendant was back with Ma. He thought he had lost it, but it found its way back again.

Like Xinying said, they were true, the stories about it, which meant the other part was true too; it will look after Ma, which means it will protect her job, which means the little master will get better. To get better he needed to have the medicine, which was ready, but they were convinced it was fatal. He had to change their minds.

There was only one way he could think of. But if it went wrong, he would be breaking a promise. A promise he made on New Year's Eve. *I'll never abandon you or give you up. I'll keep you safe, don't you worry.*

Chapter 42

But nothing would go wrong. Of course not. The pendant was returned.

"Give it to Pig," Kai said. His tone was quiet but firm, as if he were the person in charge.

"What?"

"Give it to Pig. Give some of it to my piglet." Kai fixed his eyes on Mei, then Lee, then Da Laopan.

"Kai," Mei started.

But he did not wait to hear anymore. He turned to the renovation debris and picked up a big concrete fragment. From his basket, he grabbed a shell, placed it on the ground, and dropped the concrete on it. The shell split. Kai picked up both pieces and headed straight to the pickup.

"Kai!" Mei broke into a run to his side of the truck. "Don't!"

Kai used his finger and scraped off the black layer.

"Kai, your mother said no!" Lee went round the other side.

Kai stuck his arm over the panel, his finger right in front of Pig.

"Grab hold of Pig!" Uncle Liang said.

Xinying lunged forward. At the same time, the pink tongue stuck out of the wrinkled face and wiped the black paste off Kai's finger.

"We said no!" Lee snatched the shell away. "Why do you never listen?"

All eyes were on Pig. He grunted. Then he moved toward Kai and tried to lick his finger again. He sniffed and turned his snout in Lee's direction. Next, he pottered to the end of the pickup bed where the side was dropped down. Pig tossed his head and squealed. He turned back toward Kai, who was still holding the empty shell.

"Don't let him eat anymore!" Mei said.

"Don't worry. I've got the other half." Lee raised his hand high, the inside of the shell faced everyone.

"Hang on," Da Laopan said. "Lee, look at it. The paste, its color. Yours wasn't the same."

They did not have time to consider what Laopan meant, for Pig ran along the side of the pickup bed, bashing into the bamboo, screeching.

Mei's hand clenched the fabric of her top, her knuckles white. "The poison. It's killing him!"

Kai went to the back of the truck and opened his arms. Pig ran into them. "He feels cooped up, just wants to get down. He's always like this at home. Can't sit still. Wants to get out and run." Kai felt a little contraction. "Especially when I was staying with Yee Por. I take him out every day after school, up and down the mountains."

As soon as Kai put the writhing piglet down, he ran off sniffing and grunting, covering the length and breadth of the front yard. Pig did not look like a piglet suffering or drugged. He looked revived, ready to explore this unfamiliar place.

"Thank goodness you didn't give him enough," Mei said.

"Actually," Da Laopan said. "It was the same amount as what we gave the dogs."

"Let me look at it," Ah Sau said. Nobody had noticed when she appeared. Ever since the news of Han, she had been drifting along like a ghost. Even her strong black hair had turned wispy white. "I want to see the fruit that killed my son." Ah Sau took the open shell from Lee. "I was the one who told Han not to follow the instructions. I thought I knew better. I told him one night would be enough." Like a true chef, she sniffed it. Her eyes widened. Scraping off a little, she pressed the black paste between her forefinger and thumb, as if testing the elasticity of dough.

"Can I try that?" Kai asked.

"No."

"Why can't I? I just want to see how it feels."

Ah Sau opened her palm. "Yes, of course you can feel it, just not eat it."

Kai took the paste from her and squeezed it. He rolled it forward and backward between his hands. Using both his thumbs and forefingers, he pressed the rod shape into a cube. "Ma, do you remember the raw one we opened? It was white. This is all black. Pig's eaten something different."

Pig was running round Uncle Liang, Uncle Pak, and Xinying, who had sidled away to the shady tree. His long hairy tail was swishing side to side. All eyes were on the frolicking Pig.

"There's nothing wrong with the pig." Ah Sau said.

Da Laopan finally spoke. "I can't argue with that. The piglet is very much alive. What we gave the dogs was pale brown, this paste is black." He turned back to speak in time to see Kai shove the paste into his mouth. "No, Kai!"

Chapter 43

Kai shuddered. His eyes popped. He dropped to all fours on the ground. He coughed and retched and coughed and retched. Mei and Lee squatted beside him. One on each side, they bashed his back.

"Spit it out! Spit it out!"

The coughing subsided. "That was disgusting! I'm never eating that again!"

Ah Sau chuckled. She scrapped the rest of the paste and licked her fingers. At once, she let go of the shell. She shuddered and her mouth shriveled to a thin line. She stayed frozen. Then her shoulders dropped and her eyes flew open. Her eyes made contact with everyone in the courtyard.

"Ah Sau, are you alright?"

"How do you feel?"

"Can you hear us? Ah Sau?"

"What's wrong? Tell us what's wrong?"

Then, as if a missing piece had fallen into the right place, her shoulders straightened. "I've never tasted anything like this." Ah Sau's voice was as zippy as mala sauce. "This is very strong. It's superb!" She paused. "I must say though, you might be able to feed it to Ah Fu now, but if he were any better he wouldn't have it. You've seen Kai's reaction." She moved her jaws and tongue as if it were still in her mouth. "It's too strong, but I could disguise it with chicken. It'll go well with it."

The door opened. Mrs. Laopan looked up. Da Laopan strode into the little master's room. "What happened? What was that noise outside?" Behind him, Lee, Mei, and Ah Sau stepped into the room. "Ah Sau! You look—" Mrs. Laopan searched for a suitable word.

"I feel wonderful! I've had Ah Fu's medicine."

When Mrs. Laopan was told the entire story, she could only shift her eyes from Ah Sau to Da Laopan, her face alternating between disbelief and disdain.

"Laopan couldn't have stopped me. I was going to taste it anyway, but Kai was quicker." Ah Sau paused to expel some air. "You've gone to all that trouble, the physicians, the temple, I've even lost Han—"

"Ah Sau—"

Ah Sau held up her hand. "What more have I got to lose? If

it killed me, then I can join my dead husband and son. But Kai, he followed the instructions properly and brought it all the way here. And the pig's alive. So why stop now?" Ah Sau stretched out her arms as if she were weightlifting. "But I'm still standing here, and I've never felt so energized! That antidote's purged me, cleansed me! I haven't felt this good in years! This could really be the cure. Ah Fu might really live."

Mrs. Laopan was about to reply, but her eyes flickered from Mei to Kai. "Is that your son?"

Everybody followed her eyes and turned to the doorway. Kai tried to duck.

"Yes," Da Laopan said. "Come, Kai."

Kai had no choice but to step forward. He kept his head down. For the third time that day, he had disobeyed his parents. They had told him to wait outside.

Da Laopan led him to the bed. "This is my grandson."

Kai saw a boy who was almost the same color as the clean sheets, looking like he should be in the same class as Wen or Chuan. Mrs. Laopan read his mind.

"Did you say they are the same age?" she asked Mei.

"He looks a lot younger, he's been ill for so long," Da Laopan's words tapered at the end. Then he straightened up and put both hands on his hips. "We've got to let him try it."

Mrs. Laopan's jaws were locked.

"If we don't give it to him, we know he'll…he'll…you know. What have we got to lose?"

"He'll be taken away from us even sooner!" Mrs. Laopan's voice shook.

"But he might not be. Look at Ah Sau."

"And me, I took some too."

Da Laopan waved Mei over. "Let him have it."

"Wait, what's going to happen when he takes it?"

"It will drive out his fire."

"Yes, I know that. That was what the temple man said. I was there, remember? But what will happen to him exactly?" Mrs. Laopan turned to Kai. "How did you feel when you took it?"

"It was disgusting. It was spicy and bitter and tasted like rotting meat all at the same time. I made myself vomit it out."

Ah Sau laughed. "He didn't even swallow it, it only reached the back of his mouth. But, yes, it's very strong. Even I had to close my eyes. I felt it go through my body, seeping everywhere, into my gut, under my skin. It was like chili flowing into my blood, burning my insides. Burning out all the poison."

"Ah, fight poison with poison." Laopan scanned the temple man's letter. "It says the poison will ooze out of his body."

Mrs. Laopan gave a slow nod. Mei propped Ah Fu up like a rag doll. The little master lay in her arms. Da Laopan scraped a small amount on a chopstick.

"I can't watch this." Mrs. Laopan turned away.

Kai stepped forward. "Can I do it?"

Da Laopan nodded. "But no more eating."

Kai gently pried it between the boy's pale lips. A little frown. He watched the boy so intently he did not notice someone had taken the chopstick from him until Laopan pressed it into his hand.

"Here's a bit more."

He continued to feed Ah Fu in small amounts. By the time the plate was empty, the frown was more pronounced. Kai passed the chopstick back to Laopan, who put it on the table. Kai got up and made some room for his mother. She shifted her position and eased Ah Fu into lying position. Ah Fu remained motionless on the bed. The frown was gone.

Mrs. Laopan let out a big sigh. Da Laopan took off his glasses and pressed his palm into his eyes.

Ah Fu's body twitched. His eyelids flew open. Rolling in the sockets were two ping pong balls with random black circles. His tongue stuck out to one side. His arms and legs flailed and kicked.

"Gnaaaahhhh!" he groaned.

Mrs. Laopan screamed.

Chapter 44

K ai stumbled backward. Urgent voices, raised voices, sobbing sounds crossed one another. Bodies moved about the room. Kai felt a push on his shoulders and found himself out of the room, down the corridor, and back to where the two uncles were waiting.

"Liang, can you take him back again please?" Lee's words were all strung together. He shook his head. "They're all very upset."

"Of course." Uncle Liang got up at once. "We'll go now."

They climbed back onto the truck. Mei came running out. Kai stood up.

"Ma, I'm so sorry. I shouldn't have come. I've made things worse."

Mei only shook her head, her eyes bloodshot. "Be good. Listen to Uncle Liang."

The engine roared. Kai soaked up his last image of Mei, running back to the mansion. She disappeared behind the door. He felt a cold snout on his ankles and looked down. Only then did he realize he was shaking. He would have collapsed if Xinying had not held on to him.

Chapter 45

They zoomed away from the mansion. Kai was not aware that Xinying had guided him into sitting position. Or her look of concern. Neither was he aware of Pig clattering about trying to keep his balance. He did not feel any of the jolts on the uneven road.

They rode out of the town. The open space splashed its freshness into Kai's face. Something was prodding into his thigh. He looked for the source of discomfort. The folded drawing in his pocket stuck out at an awkward position. Leaning sideways, Kai pulled it out. He had wanted to show it to Mei, to remind her of what they used to do together. Hands shaking, he unfolded it—once, twice, thrice. What would she say if she had seen it? She was always telling him to look after things so they would last. Would she sigh at the state of the paper? It was getting harder to unfold as the sheet got thinner.

Kai tried putting his thumbs between the folded leaves, but they slipped off as the pickup jolted his hands away. He tried again using his fingertips.

The pickup rolled into a deep pothole. Xinying and Kai were thrown upward. Then it rolled out of the hole. Even Pig fell over. They picked themselves up and Kai look around for the drawing. Then he spotted it.

In the distance, drifting upward, hitching a ride with the wind.

Chapter 46

Ma's drawing was gone. Ah Fu had a bad reaction. Kai had made things worse. Ma was sure to be fired now. Tears threatened to flood his eyes. Kai lifted his head toward the wind. *Let it blow them away. Don't let Xinying see I'm a baby. In fact, the wind might as well whisk me away or suck me down a long dark tunnel.*

We can all choose what we do, whether to let the setback really set us back.

Xinying's words echoed into the dark tunnel. Kai focused on them. *What would Xinying do in this situation?* A small smile crept in. *She would look for the positives however small.* Kai's mind went back to the events of last couple of days. Positives. Things that made him happy. Things that made him smile. Good things. There must be something. Were there?

He traveled here because the young master needed a cure. He knew about the young master because Ma was looking after him. Ma had left him to look after this boy. What can be good in his life? Ma abandoned him. He was left with Yee Por, who was killed in a fire. What good is there in that? Yee Por would still be alive if he had not stopped to rescue Pig. Pig. At least Pig was alive. Pig ate the paste and lived. That was a positive. Pig was alive. He had not broken his promise. He too had eaten the paste and lived. That was another positive. It was disgusting, but it was still edible. Another positive. Even when harvest was poor, he could eat it, if he were desperate enough. There were desperate days last year, and it drove Ma to leave. That morning when she left, she had given him her pendant, to keep him safe. The pendant. He'd lost it, but they'd got it back. That was a big positive. He didn't lose Ma's heirloom, despite being tricked by the ferry boy. During that crisis, Uncle Liang was kind to him. In fact, Uncle Liang had been a lot of fun when they were traveling to the Great Lake. There were baby dragons and squelchy snakes. Kai's mouth curled upward.

That night, they camped by the Great Lake again. The following morning, they made their way up the mountain.

"Ahyi, we're home!" Xinying called out.

"Lee just called."

They all froze.

"The young master woke up. He's better."

Uncle Liang picked Kai up and threw him in the air. "Did you hear that? He's alive! You saved him. Your medicine worked."

"My turn!" Wen ran toward Uncle Liang and grabbed his legs.

"No, my turn first!" Chuan hugged his other leg.

Uncle put Kai down, grabbed each twin in one arm, and spun them. After a couple of rounds, he stopped. "I'm giddy!"

The twins giggled. "Kai's turn now."

Uncle Liang squatted down to Kai's height. "Do you want to have another go? If you join us, you can always have a go. Anytime. Come and live with us."

His shining eyes gave Uncle his answer.

Chapter 47

"**K**ai?"

Kai stopped scooping the manure pile. It was a voice he had not heard for a whole month. He lifted his head to see a familiar silhouette.

"Ma! You're back! Is it your day off?" Kai threw down the spade and flung himself at her. "I'm so glad you didn't lose your job."

"Me too."

"How is the young master?" Kai asked.

"Come, it's nearly dinner time. Everyone's been asking too. I'll tell you all over dinner. But what about you, what's been happening to you?"

"I'm living with Uncle."

"I know that, what else? Anything at school?"

"Remember those horrible boys? One of them is called Jian."

"Is he giving you trouble?"

"No, not anymore. I'm not afraid of them now."

"Good. What did you do?"

"It was Uncle Bai. Jian didn't come to school often. But when he came, he always caused problems. Anyway, Uncle Bai brought Jian back to school. He spoke to Laoshi, and the school now has boarding rooms. Students can stay there all week—those who have longer walks or higher mountains to climb than us. That way they don't have to walk so far every day. But for Jian, this is great, as he's all alone now. There are people who look after him at school."

"Hasn't he got anyone?"

Kai shook his head. "His parents left when he was young. Then his grandparents died. Now his brother too, you know, the one who was killed, the one with the scar on his face, in Qiang?"

"How is he coping?"

Kai shrugged. "He has to sit next to me. He doesn't want any help, but at least he leaves me alone now."

"That's a good start."

They arrived back at Uncle Liang's.

"Looks like dinner has started."

Mei squeezed in around the table with Uncle Liang, Xinying, Kai, and the twins. She was not allowed to forget any detail of what happened after they left that day.

"Black blood came out from his ears? Ee-yr!"

"Yes, and he was burning up, really burning. I kept getting fresh water for Mrs. Laopan to wipe him all over."

"Did it cool him down?"

Mei nodded. "Just before dawn his body cooled off and his breathing steadied. Some color had returned to his face. When the sun came out, the light woke him. He opened his eyes and even managed a weak smile."

"Did he have any more of the medicine?"

Mei nodded. "But he didn't have the same reaction. The first was the worst. By the time half the seeds were used up, he was able to feed himself. When three quarters were used up, he could walk about the house by himself. He even started complaining about the strong flavor."

Uncle Liang, with his mouth full of rice, laughed so hard his faced puffed out and turned the same color as red dates.

"Fortunately, if you remember, Ah Sau knew that was going to happen. She brewed the rest with chicken. The stew was so delicious Ah Fu kept asking for it even when the antidote was long used up."

Kai beamed like a beacon. "So you can come and see us on your day off from now onward?"

"Actually, as the young master is so much better, Da Laopan wants to return to the city."

Chapter 48

The food in his mouth became twigs. "So soon?" Kai asked in a small voice.

"That's why Mrs. Laopan allowed me to come tonight. My day off is not officially until tomorrow, but they wanted to leave as soon as possible. That's why I'm here now."

"To say goodbye." Kai did not look up from his bowl.

"Yes, Kai." Mei put down her chopsticks. "So you have time to pack."

"What?"

"They want you to come back with us."

"What?"

"Kai gege's leaving?" Wen said.

Kai wished he could swallow the twigs in his mouth, but Mei answered his questions without him asking.

"Laopan said you could help Ah Sau with her chores. And if there are errands to run, you'll have to go.

"That's what—"

"Han's job was," Mei finished off his sentence.

"Kai gege doesn't have to go to school anymore?" Wen asked.

"Can I go with Kai gege too?" Chuan asked.

"The school is not ready yet, so Laopan will find a private teacher for you until it's ready."

"Private teacher?" Xinying exclaimed.

"Won't that cost money?" Kai asked.

"Yes, but Laopan is willing to pay for it."

Kai's head floated. He had dreamed of this ever since they left him with Yee Por. He glanced over at Xinying. She was staring down at the table, her hand struggling under the weight of her rice bowl. Even before Xinying looked up, Kai knew what he would see in her eyes.

Chapter 49

"You don't look very happy for someone about to be reunited with his family," Uncle Liang said.

Kai choked. "You're all my family too. What about Pig?"

"It's the city, Kai," Mei said.

Kai recognized that tone. It was the same one she used when she gave him the bad news last reunion dinner. Except this time, he was glad to hear it.

"Xinying—" Kai began.

"So is Pig leaving too?" Wen asked.

"Can we keep him?" Chuan asked.

"Xinying jie jie, ask Kai gege to let us keep Pig!" The twins chorused.

Xinying was careful not to look at Kai. She gave a small smile to the twins. "I don't make the rules in this house."

"Can we?" they turned to Uncle Liang.

"But Kai hasn't decided yet." Uncle Liang turned to Kai. "You were going to say something, before you got interrupted?"

He would not have made it through all these months without her, Kai thought. "Xinying has been such a good friend." Kai paused. "To Pig."

Xinying glanced up, her eyes like darts, but she could not stop her mouth from curling upward. He got the reaction he wanted.

"I was wondering if Xinying could look after him for me." His eyes weren't twinkling now. He did not want to be another person to leave Xinying behind. He needed to leave something special behind for her.

"Yes!" the twins cheered.

"It can stay downstairs!" Wen said.

"We can build a partition!" Chuan said.

"Only if you help," Uncle teased.

Xinying picked up a slice of mushroom. On her face was a smile so tight words could not escape from her mouth.

"That would be a lovely way for us to remember the times we had," Uncle Liang finally said. "I know Xinying will take good care of Pig for you."

Kai took one last look at the hut. His home. Not too long ago it had a stark ceiling, bare walls, and a tired wooden floor.

For the last time, he opened Pig's gate. "Come on, let's go to your new home."

For the last time, they sprinted down the path all the way to the hamlet at the bottom and to the hut at the furthest end.

"Kai gege's here!"

The twins were the first to clamber down the ladder, followed by Uncle Liang. Xinying was the last to come out.

"Xinying. Uncle Liang." Kai picked Pig up and approached Xinying. "Please look after Pig for me." Pig had doubled in size, but when he landed in her arms, she lifted in a way he had hoped. Their eyes locked. "I hope Jian will be as lucky as me, to have a friend like you."

"Don't you worry. I'm sure Xinying will take him under her wings," Uncle Liang said.

Xinying blushed. She handed Kai something wrapped in cloth. "Just a little something to remember me by."

As if he would ever forget her. His eyes stung.

"Don't open it now. It's really ugly."

"No, it's not," Uncle Liang said. "She's too modest."

Kai waved until they were out of sight, then he opened the bundle from Xinying.

Inside the parcel were two big wooden carvings—a tree and a house. The tree was three times the size of the hut. The house had stilts and a ladder leading up to the front door. Inside the house, something rattled. Kai tilted it, with the doorway over his palm. Three wooden figurines fell out. A girl, a boy, and a pig.

Acknowledgements

The idea to write this story was planted during the traditional family visits one Chinese New Year. I wouldn't have known about left-behind children if not for Tim telling me heart-breaking stories of rural people in the Chinese mountains, particularly of the six-year-old boy living on his own with only his pig. Thanks to my cousin Tan Soon Imm who told me the folklore of the Buah Keluak Tree. Also to YK, photographer extraordinaire. There are more who have helped me on this journey, from initial ideas to cooking buah keluak. You wish to remain anonymous; but you know who you are!

Members of the Singapore's Writer's Group were the first to listen to the early pages of this story. With the manuscript preparation, I acknowledge my beta readers: Lisa Tobleman, Tiziana Tabone, Rod Barclay and Melissa Menten. Thank you for your valuable feedback. For editing, I am grateful to Fran Lebowitz for pointing out the plot holes and my blind spots. Thanks also to Leah Brown for your finishing touches to the manuscript.

During the query phase I am indebted to Rena Rossner for giving her valuable time to critique my query letter and first pages. Thanks also to Beth Phelan and Peter Knapp for their work in bringing authors, publisher and agents together in #DVpit activities.

They say a picture paints a thousand words and indeed this book would not be possible without Lenny Wen's book cover and Nadège Richards' interior design.

The Singapore Arts Council organized the *Beyond Words: Young and Younger* writing competition and *The Magic Mixer* was selected as a winner. Its publication by Straits Times Press gave me the encouragement I needed to keep writing.

To Olivia at Aurelia Leo, thank you for believing in me.

To Holly, Shelley and Emily, for serving as sounding boards during the entire journey. Most of all, to Paul, for always being there.

About the Author

Justine Laismith is the winner of the *Beyond Words: Young and Younger* writing competition, who published her chapter book, *The Magic Mixer*. She grew up in Singapore and has worked in the UK pharmaceutical, chemicals, and education sectors. When not writing, she takes far too many pictures on her phone. She now lives in England.

For more information, visit:
www.justinelaismith.wordpress.com

CPSIA information can be obtained
at www.ICGtesting.com
Printed in the USA
LVHW091516051119
636416LV00007B/90/P

9 781946 024329